Greek Island Myst

(Stand-alone thri

Hotel

Murder

By Luke Christodoulou

Copyrighted Material

ALL RIGHTS RESERVED

The right of Luke Christodoulou to be identified as the Author of the Work has been asserted by him in accordance with the Copyright, Designs and Patents Act 1988.

No part of this book may be reproduced, scanned, or distributed in any printed or electronic form without permission.

This book is a work of fiction and any resemblances to persons (living or dead) or events is purely coincidental.

Published by: GreekIslandMysteries

Edited by: Dominion Editorial

Cover design: Maria Nicolaou (Mj.Vass)

Copyright © 2018 by Luke Christodoulou

Dedicated to my mother, Maria.

Thank you for reading to me...

Books by Luke Christodoulou:

The Olympus Killer (Greek Island Mystery #1) - 2014 ✓

KINDLE The Church Murders (Greek Island Mystery #2) - 2015 ✓

Death of A Bride (Greek Island Mystery #3) - 2016 ✓

KINDLE Murder on Display (Greek Island Mystery #4) - 2017 ✓

Hotel Murder (Greek Island Mystery #5) - 2018 ✓

Twelve Months of Murder (Greek Island Mystery #6) - 2019 ✗

24 Modernized Aesop Fables - 2015 ✗

Praise for the Greek Island Mysteries (Book Series):

All books in the series are rated 4-plus stars on

Amazon, Goodreads and Book Reviewing Blogs.

'The Church Murders would appeal to any reader who enjoys murder mysteries, suspenseful reads, or action adventure novels. I am pleased to recommend this book and hope that author Christodoulou is working on his next book in this promising series.'

- Chris Fischer for Readers' Favorite

'The Greek James Patterson strikes again.'

- Greek Media

'... does a masterful job writing a twisted murder story set under the Greek sun.'

- Ruth Rowley

'Greece is proud to have such a masterful writer. Death of A Bride is his best offering by far.'

- Athens Review Of Books

'Death Of A Bride is a superb murder/mystery. An Agatha Christie tale set in the 21st century.'

- National Society of the Greek Authors

'A spellbinding tale... shrouded in mystery and inflamed with revenge.'

- Elaine Bertolotti (Author)

'Great entertainment that begs to be made into a movie (...) a wealth of great stories here, well-paced and filled with believable characters, beautiful Greek imagery, fascinating insights into Greek culture and some wonderful, humorous touches. Excellent plot twists too - I really didn't see those coming. These stories can rival the bestsellers and - to be honest - the book knocks many of the famous names out of the park - an easy style, intense plot-lines, superbly lifelike characters and all this against the backdrop of gorgeous Greece and its fascinating history and culture.'

- Meandthemutts Book Reviewer

'The Church Murders is a juxtaposition of the beautiful (and gorgeously described) Greek Isles and the brutal, horrific murders that take place there.'

- Michael Young History (Author)

'Another one I could not put down.' – Jan Felton (Goodreads Reviewer)

'... meticulously crafted work. The author delivers another unique, powerful and provocative story.'

- Alex (Amazon Reviewer)

'Anxiously waiting for the next instalment!' - Jimmy Andrea (Amazon Reviewer)

'A spell-bounding thriller.' - Daniel T.A. (Author)

'As seductive as a Sudoku puzzle, the writer has crafted an ingenious plot with nothing less than stunning revelations at the conclusion.'

- Julius Salisbury (Author)

'If you like murder mysteries with great characters, atmospheric locations and a suspenseful, interesting plot to keep you turning the pages, then this book has been written for you.' –Ben (Amazon Reviewer)

'An engrossing murder mystery about a series of murders taking place on Greek islands.'

- Saritha S (Goodreads Reviewer)

'A tale of Terror! A page-turning murder mystery'.

- Sheri A. Wilkinson (Book Blog Reviewer)

'The author builds the main characters weaving them seamlessly with the plotting of a great story; even when he steps away from the present day mayhem. It's art in words at the highest pinnacle of a writer's work.'

- Rose Margaret Phillips (Book Blog Reviewer)

Chapter 1

City of Athens

It could have been another dull Tuesday. Yet, the day would go down in history as the day she murdered both her children.

Despoina Lemoni stood motionless, trapped between the dirty oven and the empty fridge; trapped in a life she no longer wished to live. The house phone hung by her side, slightly swinging by its faded-yellow, twisted cord. She could not bear to hear another word. The menacing voices roaming around her mind's darkest corners were enough noise.

'What's wrong, Mummy?' her three-year-old daughter asked, lifting her head out of her Minnie Mouse coloring book. She sat, cold and hungry, leaning on the worn-in kitchen table, wondering why her mother was sad, day in, day out. A pale ghost of a being that was once her mother. Lina raised her voice and finally caught her mother's attention.

'Nothing,' Despoina mumbled in reply, scared of the wild thoughts being born inside her head. She had not yet digested what her husband had just revealed to her.

Lina looked across the table at her infant sister. At least she always smiled at her. The nine-month-old baby happily banged her pink rattle upon the checkered blue-and-white vinyl tablecloth; both colors unable to hide the stains of ketchup, oil and other condiments that had fallen to its surface over the course of the last few months.

Five months had passed already since Despoina lost her house.

'Lost my house!' she grumbled. She hated that sentence. 'I did not *lose* my house. The bank took it away.'

Despoina gazed up and for a few serene moments looked out of her narrow basement window at the feet rushing to work on the cement pavement above; the dark clouds forming adding to their haste. Black shoes, brown shoes, flats, high heels all zoomed by her trembling, watery eyes. She craved for a job to rush to. Her Monday whining at work seemed ridiculous now. ''You never truly appreciate what you've got till it's gone,'' her Nanna used to say. Now, Despoina realized how right she was.

Soon, fat drops dived out of the grey sky and fell to the deteriorating neighborhood below. Despoina had dragged herself to the front door, and for some reason stepped out into the rain. She used to hate getting caught in the rain. The cold water sank deep into her beige blouse, while her blood seethed beneath her icy skin. All around her were signs depicting prosperity long gone. Closed shops, rundown buildings, dead trees, and piles of trash.

'Fucking crisis,' she said, the words marinated in anger and sorrow. Her fingertips ran across her face, her nails cutting into her olive complexion. Bloody rivulets quickly blossomed. She stepped back into her home, slamming the squeaking, begging-for-a-paint door behind her.

In automated 'mother-mode' she spent the rest of the evening cooking chicken nuggets and rice for her and Lina, bottle fed Antonia, bathed both girls, dressed them for sleep and put them to bed.

'Mummy?' Lina called out, watching her breath turn into a shadowy cloud, stopping her mother as she rushed to switch off her light. 'Can you tell me a fairy tale, Mummy?' she asked with hope.

'There's no such thing,' Despoina replied and left the room, mumbling how there would never be a happy ending.

Despoina raised her head high and wiped away her tears. She exhaled deeply, sure of what she had decided was needed to be done. She ambled into the kitchen and opened the top wooden cupboard, taking out a bottle of cheap, red wine. Two years ago, she would not have even used it in cooking. But that was then, and this was now. No more wine-marinated octopus and fancy food for Despoina.

Both she and her husband heard the terrifying words that petrified every parent with a mortgage. ''We are going to have to let you go''.

Despoina fell back into her ripped armchair, pushing her dying-for-a-dye blonde hair over the top of its burgundy back. She brought the wine to her lips as she turned on the radio. Love songs and rain. She always loved the combination. With eyes forcibly shut, she daydreamed of moments lived, yet vanished into oblivion. Paradise lost. That's what the Greeks had, according to her.

Window-shaking thunder startled her. She had dozed off. An hour had passed since the last drop of fruity wine. Brought-up religiously, Despoina had no doubt about the eternity of the soul. Life on earth was a mere blip on the line of our existence.

'It's for their own good. I will not have them eating trash and being ridiculed about their father...' she whispered, lifting herself out of the rocking armchair.

With slow steps, she approached the kitchen sink and splashed frigid water upon her sallow face. She dawdled back to her children's door. Each step was harder to make. In her trembling right hand, she held her heavy pillow. Without another bedroom in the hole-of-a-house, she slept on the living room sofa.

Her hand froze upon the shiny door knob. Despoina closed her eyes and sighed as she quietly opened the door. The lone light came from a Disney princess night lamp. Placed on the floor between the bed and the cot, it cast a dim, pink glow; just about enough light for Despoina to see her sleeping babies. She sat by Lina and gently caressed her hair; her mind splicing heavy knots in her alcohol-filled stomach.

'I love you, my beautiful,' she managed to utter, her throat clogging up. The pillow came down hard on Lina's small face. The young girl awoke, unable to breathe. Despoina kept both hands on the pillow and pushed down, while looking away. Soon, the girl's kicks ceased, and silence returned to the dark room.

Three hours to bring her into the world and three minutes to take her out of it.

Antonia was next and in less time, followed the fate of her lifeless sister.

The first rays sailed from the timid, winter sun and reached the bedroom window, forcing the darkness to shrivel into shadows. The two dead girls lay in their beds. Eternal sleep, offered by the hands of the woman that brought them to life. Down the narrow hallway, another body sat against the chipped, riddled with mold wall.

Despoina had loaded her husband's hunting rifle, prayed to the Lord for forgiveness and brought the cold gun barrel to her quivering chin. She closed her eyes, and as her last tear journeyed down her cheek, Despoina found the courage to pull the trigger. A film-noir fan, she always joked about how she wanted to go out with a bang.

The police found her with her head blown open, yet with a smile permanently frozen on her. The wall behind her was sprayed with crimson blood and parts of her tormented brain. She hated that wall. Poetic revenge, she would have called it.

The neighbors gathered in shock and watched as the paramedics carried out the tiny lifeless body of Antonia, the body of the happy girl next door – Lina's golden locks blowing in the wind out from beneath the white sheet-, and the bloody body of the woman who would haunt their everyday conversations. They were also struggling. The economic crisis had brought them all to their knees.

Despoina's acts of death caused daily riots and fueled the anger against the government's strict austerity program. Her murderous ways were analyzed by 'experts' of every kind. Newspapers, news, blogs all featured the story.

But, like every tragedy in history, it became exactly that. History. People moved on to the next hot topic of the month, and new austerity measures kept being announced.

Chapter 2

Valentina stared at her phone's screen in amazement. Her alarm was set to go off in just nine minutes. *Great. Dear brain, thank you! Thank you for keeping me up all night thinking of things that I worry about all day.*

She rubbed her tired eyes as the illuminating light from her cell died out and pitch black governed the room once more. Sleepily, she kicked back the heavy, mint-green quilt, hoping to fight off the drowsy heat invading from the wall radiator. Turning to her side, her hand brushed against Alexandro's bare back. She still could not get used to having a man in her house, in her life, in her heart. She hugged his naked body from behind and breathed in his 'man-smell'. She never could find the right title for it. He was her first; she had no other 'naked, sleeping man smell' to compare it to. She gently laid her lips upon his neck and reluctantly slid out of the king size bed. She tiptoed to the door, avoiding the parade of her shoes in front of the wooden wardrobe. She needed to take nothing. She had taken her make-up, clothes and shoes into the living room, the night before. Alexandro worked late, interrogating suspects in a case involving manslaughter at a nightclub while she was on duty with the crack of the Greek dawn. Being a parking enforcement officer was as boring as it sounds, yet Valentina did not mind the long shifts in all weather conditions, handing out tickets and arguing with vexed Athenian drivers. She was in the big city, away from her rock-of-an-island, and she had the whole package. An apartment, a job and a man.

Forty minutes later, a uniform-wearing Valentina walked out the front door; her platinum blonde hair rolled-up into a bun, her lips graced with bright-red lipstick and her stomach filled with two pieces of bread, covered in Nutella, and a sizzling hot, milky coffee.

She locked the stained chestnut, fiberglass door and sighed. Before her eyes, once again hung a metallic six. Valentina turned the number upright again and pushed down with force. Apartment nine's only issue - the unscrewed number.

'Let's remind Alex, once again, to fix it,' she whispered the mental note, her mind laughing at the image of the mug she had bought him on a weekend escape. 'When a man says he will fix it, he'll fix it. No need to remind him every six months,' was written in bold, black letters across the large, white cup.

*****

Not so far away, in the neighborhoods on the other side of the Parthenon, I was also creeping out of my apartment. Nothing worse than the fury of an awoken-before-her-time American, short-fused spouse.

I stood in front of the dirty, hall mirror. The reflection staring back at me was finally one that caused me to smile. After a long two-year battle with cancer, I had started to gain weight –not too hard taking into account my undying love for street food and red meat; my color had returned to a healthy Greek white, and short, thin, brown hair had appeared back on my scalp, helping to shake off the unattractive image of my egg-shaped head. Most bald men look sexy; I looked like Humpty Dumpty's not-so-well-known, Greek cousin.

Ioli Cara's phone call had abruptly popped my dream bubble - me standing between Messi and Ronaldo, celebrating with our fans, the top three soccer players in the world. Age fifty and still certain dreams remained the same. Though, back then, it was Maradona and Platini by my side.

'Sorry, boss, for waking you. I just got the fax from Interpol. The old guy had hidden property across Greece. All under fake names. Typical businessman avoiding taxes. There is a remote mansion in the meadows of Rhodes listed. Remember how his wife mentioned that he loved Rhodes as a child and that is why he built Anastos Tower by Rhode's port? I'm thinking if Scrooge is hiding out somewhere, this is the place. If he is not there, he is abroad. With money like his, he would need no passport.'

'You talk too much. How long have you been up?'

'An hour or so. Babies don't feed themselves, you know? Icarus has a Cretan appetite and an inner clock more precise than a Swiss watch,' she replied laughing.

'Okay, okay...' I had replied, jumping out of bed and rushing to the bathroom. Safe from Tracy's icy looks, I told Ioli to arrange the police ferry.

'Wait. Are we not sending local police? Is it worth us going out there on a hunch?'

'The fresh sea air will do us good. Besides, even if he is not there, we have no warrant. I'd rather it be just the two of us.'

'So, we enter illegally, Captain Costa, Mr. Moral, Papacosta?'

'Well, if there was a suspicious sound coming from within...'

Ioli laughed again, and a light cry was heard from her infant son. 'Oh, no. The monster is moving. I'd better get out of here. Leave him to Mark. See you at headquarters,' she said hastily and the phone went silent.

Our case was not exactly *homicide-team material*, but three point seven billion to your name gets you attention. The chief placed half the task force on the case of the missing billionaire. Thanasis Zampetides, Greece's shipping tycoon, aged seventy-two had vanished. His children reported him missing in a matter of hours. That was forty-three days ago. Most presumed the worst. The chief wanted no 'fuck-ups' as he so elegantly put it. He had the minister's office breathing down his neck, and he wanted to make sure that if the old guy's body turned up, his best officers were on the case.

Weeks of searching by police and private investigators, and unlimited airtime and press space offered zero results.

Ioli's gut instinct had always helped us solve cases in the past. Ioli felt certain that Mr. Zampetides, for reasons unknown, was taking time away from his hectic world of running Greece's largest shipping company. Having read through his biography, and after interviewing his wife, she was sure that the missing billionaire –as a free spirit, a child of the 60s- was somewhere relaxing. The police had eliminated the possibility of kidnapping as the security cameras showed him leaving his Athenian skyscraper alone and no ransom demands had ever been made.

To be completely honest, though intrigued by the mysterious lack of evidence, I did not deposit much of my time into the case. I had a pile of paperwork to attend to before my paper tower surpassed Pisa's as the world's tallest leaning tower, I had two court appearances to prepare for, and I preferred cases closer to home. The butchered homeless man behind Omonoia's square was far more deserving of my attention.

Ioli though needed to silence her gut. She began investigating places the billionaire could be. And with her known determination, fast forward forty-three days later, and we were set for the spear-shaped island of Rhodes.

Chapter 3

The crisp winter night succeeded the short, rainy winter day and Valentina returned home, hungry, exhausted and soaking wet.

'What a shitty day,' she said as she kicked off her black shoes, offering much-needed relief to her swollen ankles. 'That's how honest money is made, Valentina,' she mimicked her father's deep bass voice. New to the force, she was the lowest ranking officer on traffic department's totem pole. With the austerity measures holding back any hope for new recruits, she knew well that long shifts and busy streets would always be assigned to her. She also knew that in today's Greece having any sort of job was a blessing, so Valentina kept her whining to herself.

Closing the heavy door and leaving the outside world behind her, her eye caught a glimpse of a shiny, magnolia envelope that lay on the scratched, laminated flooring. Bending down, she picked it up and flipped it around. Fancy, bold red letters covered its side.

Hotel Murder.

'The mystery weekend experience of a lifetime,' Valentina read the smaller subtitle. The next line though was the one that caught her attention. 'Congratulations! You have won a FREE stay. Please open.'

Valentina's red nails slid into the paper, ripping the envelope open.

'Congratulations,' the letter wished once more.

'You are holding one of the thirty random invitations to the grand opening of Hotel Murder. This is an ambitious project, looking to make its mark on Greece's tourist map. A remote hotel, with five-star amenities, upon a majestic Greek Isle. With multiple actors and a devilishly, cunning mystery, it is destined to entertain you.

For our first weekend, we have decided to offer thirty lucky winners a FULLY FREE stay. No strings attached what-so-ever. No hidden charges. Free transfer from Piraeus port, free stay, all meals and drinks 100% free, and free participation in the mystery. All we want is your opinion.

So, what are you waiting for? Bring your PLUS-ONE (also FREE – yes, the boss has gone crazy!) to Piraeus port on Friday 2nd of December, 16:00 sharp. Return to Piraeus, Sunday night.

Still a disbeliever? Too good to be true?

Call for inquiries: 01 3478 9812.'

Valentina read the letter twice. *Too good to be true'*

She placed the envelope on her prized possession, an antique coffee table, similar to the one her Nana had in the house she grew up in, back on her home island of Folegandros. She rubbed her shoulders and walked into her bedroom. A hot, steamy bath was all she could focus on for the time being. She shed off her work clothes and slid into the shower. Water dangerously close to boiling point attacked her skin, providing warmth to her body. She spread coconut shower gel across her neck and chest, sniffing the mesmerizing aroma.

Fifteen minutes later, she drifted into the kitchen, comfortable pyjamas covering her relaxed, slender figure. Now, all she needed was a good, strong Greek coffee to complete her after-work nirvana. With the blinds up, Valentina curled up on her bright magenta sofa and, with her coffee entrapped between her warm fingers, she stared out at the rain. Soon, the first sips travelled down her, warming her from the inside. Unwound, her attention fell to the Hotel Murder invitation.

Alexandro would love it, she thought. *Men and their mystery stories!*

She must have heard over a dozen times, Alexandro's retelling of how he cracked the case at a murder/mystery dinner in England while visiting a cousin. He was only eighteen at the time. Now, a homicide officer, she could picture him diving in and analyzing everything. She thought the whole idea sounded corny, but then again, *the things women do for their men.* And with that thought, she guzzled her hot beverage and took her phone into her hands.

One beep, two beeps... 'Hello?' a fruity, youthful voice came through the receiver.

'Er, yeah. I found an invitation under my door... Hotel Murder?' she asked.

'Congratulations! Welcome to an experience of a lifetime...'

And the horrific acting begins, Valentina could not resist thinking and interrupted the eager-to-inform employee. 'Yes, yes. So, it's completely free?'

'One hundred percent, ma'am. Just bring your invitation and if your invitation specifies it, your plus-one. The ship will be expecting you at 16:00 sharp, Friday 2nd of December.'

'Yes, I've already read that part. What island is the hotel on?'

'That is part of the mystery,' the surely-under-twenty-five-year-old man said.

'You serious? We won't know where we are heading?' Valentina said, bringing her knees up to her chest, placing her cold feet under the couch pillows.

'Rules of the management. They want to avoid people intruding the weekends. The storyline begins the moment you set foot on board. It will be an amazing...'

'Yeah, yeah. I'm sure. Okay, count us in. What details do you need for the reservations?'

'None. Just bring your invitations. Your identities and back-stories will be provided by a member of staff. See you on the dock next Friday. We are dying to meet you. Pun intended!'

Oh, God. And the nightmare begins'

Alexandro and his muddy boots came home an hour later. Valentina stopped him at the door with a passionate kiss and a warning about his footwear.

'Mmm, what smells so freaking good?' he said, his droopy, Greek nose opening its narrow nostrils like a hound dog on a mission. 'My baby been cooking?' he inquired as his arms reeled her closer and his wide hands explored her rear.

'You wish. After the day I've had, you're lucky I got up to greet you,' she replied, the corners of her lips travelling upwards. 'I ordered pork chops from that tavern you talk about more than me...'

'Meat Castle?' he interrupted her, his voice climbing the decibel scale fuelled by excitement and an empty stomach.

'That's the one,' Valentina replied as she was raised up into the air. Alexandro lowered her gently and laid a forceful kiss on her slightly cracked-from-the-cold lips. Nothing that a few drops of virgin olive oil could not fix; Valentina remembered her mama's home remedy.

'Love truly does pass from the stomach,' she said and laughed as Alexandro rushed to the wooden IKEA table.

Valentina enjoyed their dinner time - her favorite time with Alexandro. A workaholic and a 'gymaholic', his appetite was greater than any man she had ever met. She watched him over their candle-lit meals as he relished all sorts of meats. Valentina was not very fond of the kitchen, while he was an able cook. The nights he did not 'create' –his verb for his cuisine masterpieces- Valentina prepared something simple along the lines of spaghetti or burgers, or ordered from an array of choices. Neither of them was a fussy eater. With delight, she witnessed him calm down from his hectic day and smiled as he retold his daily adventures; she even laughed at his rather unamusing jokes.

Finally, plates were licked clean, and the last drop of Merlot travelled down his throat.

'I've got another surprise for you,' Valentina said, and an enigmatic smile came to life below her round, glover-green eyes.

'What's that, babe?' he replied, relaxed with his voice tone carrying the vast satisfaction his body was experiencing.

'Next Friday, you and I, a murder/mystery weekend on an island. What do you say to that, mighty detective?'

Alexandro tilted his head slightly to the right and studied his girlfriend with the same manner he 'read' suspects down at the station.

'You for real?'

'Realler than your love for Olympiakos,' she replied, unable to control her high-pitched laughter. 'God, talk about murdering proper grammar.'

'That's, err, great,' he said and got up to take his vacant plate to the sink.

'Why so unenthusiastic?' Valentina inquired, picking up the hesitant color in his words.

'No, no, Don't get me wrong. I just... well, not to sound like a party pooper, but can we afford this? I mean, Christmas is just around the corner, and I paid for all that shit to be fixed on my car last month...'

'Ssshh,' Valentina said, walking over to him and placing her index finger on his moving lips. 'You worry too much. Stress will be the death of you. I know our financial capabilities well. I won this weekend. It is completely free.'

His face lit up and his eyes opened wide. 'Seriously?'

'Yep, all-inclusive. Will not cost us a dime.'

Valentina swore that all the neighbors heard his cowboy yell of celebration and the loud kisses he placed on her lips and neck.

An hour later, Alexandro exited the shower, dried off and remained naked as he climbed into bed next to her. Valentina kept her eyes glued to her romance book, yet could not concentrate on the words blurring up before her. She knew well what was coming. His hands teased her by invading under her bedtime T-shirt. She turned to look at him. She loved that goofy expression; his mischievous grin upon his flushed face. He knew all her buttons. In seconds, Nora Roberts fell to the floor, followed by her underwear and purple T-shirt. His tongue, travelling from her belly upwards, sent shivers down her spine and shook her inner core. Though her only lover,

Valentina believed they had great chemistry. When in her, she felt sexier than any romance heroine. Later, she drifted off to sleep in his broad arms, beaming and content. Soon, both departed for dream land and visions of a spectacular and bewildering mystery weekend came to life in their mind's inner cinema.

Chapter 4

With relief, I felt the police ferry swirl upon the restless Aegean Sea and gradually come to a halt, gently hitting its side upon the soft, pitch-black, truck wheels hanging from the cracked cement pier. The 'non-tourist' pier needed no color nor decorations. Used only by local fishermen and the coastguard, it paled next to its big brother, the impressive harbor of Rhodes; welcoming some of the world's largest cruise ships.

The calendar read December, and both harbors stood relatively silent. The mayhem of summer was a distant memory set to replay all over again in a few months.

My feet settled on solid ground. My stomach took longer. The icy winter breeze of the sea caressed and chilled my skin. I breathed in the fresh air and smiled as Ioli jumped off the ferry and landed beside me.

'What's wrong, boss? Sea nausea?' she asked, her hands fixing her silky, black hair back into a high ponytail. 'I hope not. You're scared of planes; I need you to cope with ferries,' she continued without waiting for a reply.

'Yeah, yeah. Tease the old guy. The sea was rough, today. I love the ferry, don't I?' I asked, turning to comically stroke our trusted boat.

Ioli refrained from commenting, rolled her eyes and paraded down the deserted pier.

'How's little Icarus doing?' I managed to ask, short of breath as I ran to catch up, closing my brandy-brown jacket right up to the last button. The last thing I needed was a cold.

'The *little terrorist of love* has put us in Christmas-mode. Can you believe it? Me. Decorating the house with bright lights, putting up a tree and buying him a shit-load of toys?'

'It happens to the best of us,' I replied with a smile. 'I know you hate the whole jolly season, but deep down, you secretly crave for it. We all do, and a kid is the perfect excuse.'

'The woman next door said the same. She misses her kids as babies. Kids grow faster than weeds, she said, and just like weeds, they find themselves in places they shouldn't be. Just wait till he begins to walk, she warned me. Oh, the joys that await me,' Ioli continued, rather out of her normally quiet self. I guessed long hours at home, alone with an infant makes you chatty.

Ioli was still talking about her son as we entered the rental-car shop, located next to a closed-for-the-winter ice-cream parlor. Further down the quiet street, an alluring cafe with its chairs situated between two burning-bright fireplaces was the only other shop with signs of life. A hot-chocolate mixed with coffee sounded divine. Maybe on our way back.

The senior lady behind the tall, glass counter welcomed us with a bored grunt of 'Good morning' and with a push of her slipper-wearing feet, she rolled back with her office chair towards the wall decorated with numbered car keys. Watching her fill in the needed paperwork was duller than watching olives being picked by my Aunt Toula. With a flat line smile on her downcast face, she handed us the necessary key and a few unnecessary words of advice on how to drive safely.

'Giving birth took less time,' Ioli joked as she sat in the passenger's seat and cracked her knuckles. Shortly, we were driving through the old, dark-ages-built part of the city of Rhodes. The impressive castle walls ran up to the cloudy sky on our left while deep, dark blue sea filled our view to the right.

'Jelly baby or gummy bear?' Ioli asked, waving her two small bags of candy. She had already eaten two by the time she offered me one.

'Neither, thanks,' I replied, still searching for my favorite radio station.

'Can you see the village?' I asked Ioli as I stopped at the next T-junction. Multiple signs stood before us, the letters hard to read due to sprayed-on football slogans. An unwanted gift by the local hooligans.

'There,' she replied, pointing at the metallic tree of road signs. 'Kamiros Skala, thirty-one kilometers. Turn right.'

Ioli sat with her hands folded in her lap and her gaze focused on the sun rays dancing upon short-lived, loud waves. My attention remained on the narrow, country road unfolding before my tired eyes. Late nights and early mornings were not something my five-decade-old body was willing to put up with. At least, continuously. I never did have trouble sleeping. Even through my life's plentiful stressful situations, I slept like a cub in its mother's paws. Now, with nothing major to bother my mind, I seemed to find it impossible to turn off the voices and fall peacefully to Morpheus' land. I don't know about sheep, but I can number the lighting-shaped cracks on my bedroom's ceiling and walls. I could even number the times I felt guilty for craving a cigarette. All. I quit so many years ago and still yearn to feel a bud on my lips and smoke journeying down my throat. But a promise is a promise. I swore to my daughter that I would never smoke again and with her in Heaven watching down on me, I would not let my sleepless boredom win and disappoint my Gaby for a harmful, brief pleasure. I thought about pills. I thought about drinking. Both dangerous ideas with my addictive behavior.

'You're awfully quiet, today.' Ioli's smooth voice interrupted my galloping thoughts.

'Just tired, I guess,' I replied as I turned from the main artery and entered a neglected country road. A few scattered houses broke the natural background of stubborn, twisted olive trees, wheat fields and trees filled with bright-yellow lemons. No souls lingered on the neglected sidewalks or in the flower-filled gardens. The smoke twirling out of the brick chimneys revealed that their tenants hid from Boreas' icy blows. The thin mist gathering in the valley was not inviting either.

'Can I take a wild guess on the house of Thanasis Zampetides?' Ioli asked with a grin and a raise of her thin eyebrows.

A country manor stood out from the rest. At least, the part of it that was taller than the brick wall and the sky-reaching pine trees that were planted on the inside, along the wall. The impressive gate still looked grand, though rusty. No smoke exited from the four chimneys that came into view as I brought the rental to a halt, feet from the gate. Ioli opened her door and paused at the sight of shallow muddy puddles.

'Let me hop out and open the gate...' I began to say, ready to put the gear into P.

Ioli slightly shook her head. 'No, Peppa Pig's got this. At least, it isn't raining.'

I watched as she plodded among the watery minefield and pushed back the heavy gate with ease. I slowly drove up beside her and waited for her to wipe her navy-blue Jodhpur boots with a lavender-scented baby wipe. The broad gravelled driveway sliced the vast, neglected garden into two. The mansion, though in better condition than the surrounding grounds, showed signs of abandonment. The hot summers in alliance with the cloudy, rainy winters had attacked viciously the house's once-white paint. The wood-work suffered, also.

'You still sure we are going to find something here?' I dared to ask as I stepped out of the car and approached the wooden front door.

'Only one way to find out,' she mumbled in reply and pressed the doorbell button.

An irritating buzzing sound echoed from inside the house. We waited in silence. Ioli pressed again.

'What happened to nice, friendly ding-dongs?' I commented upon hearing the awful buzzing sound once more.

'Okay, a walk around the house it is,' Ioli said and trudged off, checking every window as she went. Each of them, tightly locked. I rubbed the frost and dirt off the windows, yet nothing was visible inside. Thick, burgundy curtains hid the stomach of the house well.

Thunder called out to us, warning us of the intentions of the gathering clouds above. Sunlight weakened, and shadows grew stronger. Thankfully, the back porch door was unlocked. Ioli took the cold handle into her leather glove and pushed back the door.

'Oh, for the love of God...' Ioli said, covering her nose. The musty air carried a putrid scent. A shadow moved with speed upon hearing her footsteps. Ioli cursed again and jumped at the sight of the dead-rat dangling from an alert cat's blood-dripping mouth. The

Bengal cat took one cautious look at us and vanished in seconds from the study.

More rattling noises were heard from inside the manor.

'More cats?' Ioli whispered and placed her right hand upon her firearm.

'Let's hope so,' I said and called out, 'Hellenic Police. Is anybody, here?'

My voice bounced around the room, causing clattering from the next room. From the open door, the Chesterfield sofa betrayed the nature of the room. We cautiously entered the living room. Ioli had her gun raised to chest level, while I took heavy, slow steps towards the armchair facing the majestic fireplace. A few well-fed rats scattered into dark corners as I approached the beige, tall-back chair. To my bad luck, their stubborn leader remained. I gingerly placed my sweaty hand upon the chair's arm and swirled it around. A decomposing, old, short man faced me accompanied by a chubby rodent feasting on his face. The pack of rats had nibbled half his face off. I did the sign of the cross upon my body and took a step back as the rat king showed his crimson painted teeth at me, before leaping from the dead body and rushing off to his loyal troops of scavengers.

Chapter 5

Valentina arrived at the port at the only time she knew - late.

No matter the effort, it seemed she never managed to keep a schedule and be where she had to be, the time she had to be.

Alexandro walked with a fast pace in front of her, one arm behind his back, rolling his black suitcase along, the watch-wearing other arm raised to eye level.

'Shit, it's twenty past.'

'So? The invitation said four. I doubt the boat has left...'

'There might be a presentation or something,' Alexandro cut her sentence as he paused to look around. His head turned from left to right, and his wary eyes scanned the vast port of Piraeus.

'How the heck are we supposed to know where to go?' he asked with hints of desperation coloring his voice. Tens of ships stood proudly before him, towering him, standing perfectly still, though on water. The frail winter breeze, known for its chilly bite by the sea, did not carry the strength to move these eight thousand tonne steel commercial ships.

'Relax, hon. It won't be here. It will be further down. Ferries are after the cruise ships,' Valentina said, walking straight past him and turning left down the long ocean-side road. 'And I'm supposed to be the girl from out of town!'

'You sure?' Alexandro replied, paying no attention to her pun.

Valentina took off her red woolly hat, and her blonde hair escaped, free to dance upon the wind. A smile came to life upon her face as her eyes noticed a bright yellow board with crimson red capital letters dominating its top. HOTEL MURDER, it read.

'Told you so,' she said, gloating.

Alexandro rushed to the sign, mumbling as he read. 'Dock, 52. Passenger area,' he finally said clearly, and speedily continued down the road, zig-zagging among tired-looking workers carrying tools and buckets towards an aging ship, covered in blisters and peeling paint. The relentless Greek sun showed no mercy to all beneath it during prolonged summer periods.

Valentina did her share of mumbling as well. 'Couldn't have grabbed a taxi or the Metro to the main entrance? No, we had to bring our own car and leave it in the furthest parking lot possible 'cause it's cheaper... It's a free trip for God sake...' she grumbled from behind closed teeth. Luckily for them both, Alexandro's pointy ears were too far away to catch any of her displeased words.

The line for the Hotel Murder ferry stood out from the rest like a black olive in a piece of pie. Plain docking rails were lowered from smaller ships that ran the routes back and forth from the Greek Isles connecting islanders and the handful of tourists with the capital. Small island airports which maintained operations during the three winter months were scarce.

The boarding area for the Hotel Murder ferry was anything but plain.

For their guests, staff had prepared and were serving fancy canapes on silver platters, a red carpet lay on the cold, grey cement ground and a lavish rail connected land with the freshly painted speed-boat. The colorful ferry stood out among the dull-painted rest. Stripes of bright red, blue and yellow travelled around it; it was as bright as a spring riot of freshly born flowers.

Alexandro took one look at the crowd waiting to board the boat and turned to Valentina's direction. 'You sure we are invited? Seems like an upper-class crowd kind of thing.'

Valentina had her eyes on her jacket's zipper as she opened the blue, thick sports jacket, offering herself cool air. Running behind Alexandro worked up quite a sweat. She had already regretted her beige cashmere jumper. Valentina's emerald eyes gazed up and studied the well-dressed group of people chatting away carefree around three tall tables, drinking champagne.

'Guess the crisis is not for all,' Alexandro whispered as he, too, unzipped his black, leather jacket.

'Just because they're dressed-up...' Valentina began to say, yet was interrupted by a man in his early thirties –maybe even younger, dressed in full sailor's outfit, standing on the edge of the ferry, looking down at the covering of around twenty people.

'Ladies and gentlemen, your attention please,' the fair-haired man began his speech, adding extra bass to his voice. The chattering fell down the decibel scale all the way to complete silence. Even the bombshell blonde jabbering about her loft in Switzerland to two ladies, both in their late fifties, stopped the conversation immediately and swung her stool in the direction of the voice.

'Welcome to the experience of a life time. Again, congratulations on your win. I am Platonas Pappas. On behalf of Hotel Murder, I welcome you on board. The staff and I, are at your service. Your luggage is being loaded as we speak...'

Valentina smiled politely at the young man that ran up to them and discreetly took their suitcases.

Platonas raised a handful of envelopes in the air and continued his passionate oration. 'I have here an envelope for every one of you. I ask you to study everything enclosed meticulously. You will find your new identity for the weekend, your character's background details and more. Please, do not, I repeat, do not share anything written in red. Those details are to be known later on in the game. After the first murder!'

'New identity?' a bull-necked man with greasy, jet-black hair pondered out loud.

'First murder? Oh, sounds so exciting,' the youngest of the group, a twenty-something, pale-skinned girl said excitingly, turning to her two brothers, standing by her side.

'It's not as complicated as it sounds,' Platonas replied and let his high-pitched awkward giggle slip through the words. 'You will use your real first name. It is mostly details needed to help move the game along.'

Just then, a coltish man with a distinct Greek nose and a row of dazzling, white teeth stepped forward.

'As we are in a questioning mood, may I ask what I believe is on everyone's mind?'

'Food?' Alexandro whispered into Valentina's ear and followed his quip with a kiss on her icy earlobe. Valentina smiled and leaned into him, while the gentleman with the posh manner of speaking continued with inquiring where exactly their destination was.

'Yeah,' the only man wearing jeans besides Alexandro shouted in agreement. 'Where are we going? You lured us in with your free offer of luxury and mystery, and failed to mention where the heck you're taking us,' the scruffy looking, thick-bearded man continued, chewing up the words as he spoke, leaving behind various vowels.

'See? It's not just royalty,' Valentina said into Alexandro's ear and returning his previous gesture with a full-lip kiss on his freshly-shaved neck.

Platonas coughed quietly and looked straight at the man complaining. 'My dear sir, the unknown destination is a part of the mystery,' he said, maintaining his professional tone. 'And, between us, I think the company wants the focus to be the hotel and the experience and not the island. You know, if they said it was Skiathos, people would be like, oh, I've been there before, or I don't like Skiathos, it's too commercial and so on. You will not be experiencing the island. It's a two-day game. But, trust me, it will be amazing,' he continued, now more casually, taking on a friendly tone as he noticed his original answer did not register well.

'Well said, my lad,' a fruity voice came from behind them. A plum, six feet tall Bishop approached, dressed in his pitch black clerical clothing. His heavy, pure gold chain with a diamond-decorated cross was the only item breaking the darkness of his attire. 'I am Bishop Arsenios. Sorry, I'm late,' he added, his eyes gathering in their corners and forming a judgmental look, aimed at his petite wife who breathlessly followed him. Her thin figure was covered by a dark purple dress and despite her not being older than forty, white hairs danced out of her strict bun. 'Oh, and this is my wife, Salome.'

Salome offered a flat smile from her make-up free face and quickly lowered her dark hazel eyes.

Platonas also had his head lowered listening to a young, red-haired girl with a block of papers in her hands. Valentina studied her hands; she counted eight rings on her slender fingers. As she lifted her gaze from the girl's turquoise nail polish, she read her lips. *'That's all of them.'*

Platonas stood soldierly, a posture he performed well during his short stint in the army, and proudly announced: 'Ladies and gentlemen, you may board the ferry. Hotel Murder awaits you!'

Chapter 6

Lights came to life upon the luxurious ferry as guests eagerly boarded. Bright light covered the wooden deck and illuminated the lounge area of the boat. The sun was still lingering above the oceanic horizon, and a full moon dominated the sky, yet nature's lustre carried no power.

Valentina slid her hand into Alexandro's and moved slowly behind the two near-senior ladies. Her thoughts running back to Folegandros and her dear mother. She, also, would have worn her best fur coat, wore a tad of make-up too much and had her hair blown up in the same style as the two friends who seemed to be walking slower than a zombie in a George Romero movie.

'I'll be their age by the time we board,' Alexandro jokingly said, leaning closer to her; his warm breath was in contrast to the chilly wind that was growing in strength as the sun began to dip into the Aegean.

Valentina kicked his foot and her lips took on what Alexandro kindly referred to as her 'fish-face'. Yet, her signature, prolonged 'Shh,' never came. Her googly eyes were pointing to the lady's black shades. Alexandro's deductive mind took over and even though the lanky woman had no walking cane or behaved in any obvious way as visually impaired, he realized she was blind. Her steps were taken carefully, while her left hand held tightly to the railing. The tip of her shoe caught his attention. Like an Indian scout, it moved ahead charily in search of hazardous obstacles.

'Small step ahead, dear,' her friend said, as the duo reached the end of the three-meter railing, serving as a bridge between land and transport to an unknown destination. Her right hand hovered as she paused and waited to feel her friend grab her and take the step with her.

'I'd rather lose all my other senses than sight,' Valentina whispered, mostly talking to herself, releasing inner thoughts of phobias carried over a lifetime.

'Logical,' Alexandro replied with a mischievous grin. 'How could you live without gazing at this marvelous face and body?' he asked, stretching out his arms and flexing his muscular build.

'My Apollo!' Valentina said, taking on a school-play, theatrical tone of voice.

'Huh? Did you call me?' the gentleman standing a few feet behind them inquired. 'Have we met before?' he continued in a shaky voice.

'Excuse me?'

The man read her expression. 'Nothing. Sorry,' he rushed to apologize. 'Just thought I heard my name. I was distracted by the beauty of the sun setting and thought you called me. I'm Apollo,' he said and took a lengthy step forward, extending his hand towards their direction.

Valentina swallowed a raging giggle and shook his cold hand.

'Valentina,' she replied and introduced Alexandro.

'You seem like a lovely couple,' he said with a wide smile. He then tilted his black Fedora hat with a pinch of his fingers and rushed past them into the warmer belly of the boat.

Valentina and Alexandro exchanged a silent, short-lived kiss on their dry, icy lips and followed. Soon, both sank back into the soft sofa in the corner of the lounge; lost in each others arms. Waiting in silence and excitement for their weekend getaway to begin.

'Quite a blend of people,' an olive-skinned man, with wide shoulders and a well-cared-for mustache, commented as he sat down beside them. He leaned forward, placing his elbows upon his legs and was first to rip open the white envelope provided to all passengers as they boarded. As his bright, pale-gold eyes skimmed over the letter with the fine print and the Hotel Murder seal, Valentina studied his grayish hairs as they fought against his chestnut hairs for dominance on his skull.

'It's him,' she said, finding herself whispering in her man's ear once again.

'Who?' Alexandro replied without turning, in his 'I'm listening, but not really paying attention' voice that she despised. She caught his eyes pretending to be journeying carefree around the low ceiling room, yet she knew he focused on the bombshell who had settled opposite them - her breasts and rear ready to burst out of her shockingly tight dress. Valentina did not mind him staring. Her eyes were not faithful either, during most days. Valentina had a rule. Well, it was more of a saying. You can look at the menu, you just cannot order.

She placed her hand upon his strong chin and turned him in her direction. 'Theodore Moutsina, the congressman you made me vote for during the last election.'

Alexandro spun round immediately, ignoring Valentinas's nails as they gently scraped his barely noticeable beard. 'Sir? Oh, it is a pleasure to meet you. We vote in Athens' A District and are avid supporters. We are police officers and your stance on crime…'

Theodore's uproarious laughter cut his flow of admiration.

'Calm down, son,' he said and took Alexandro's right hand, sandwiching it in both of his. His trademark handshake. 'Glad to meet supporters, but please, no politics. Here, I am…' He took a look at his papers and continued 'Theodore, the retired gardener that will stay in room 103 and discover the second murder weapon in the library on the second day'.

He winked at Valentina and said, 'I'll say no more. I plan to win this game and having two officers of the law against me, just makes this all that much harder. I love solving mysteries!'

As Alexandro continued his conversation with his political hero, Valentina took her own envelope into her hands, cut the edge and slid her nail inside. She leisurely ripped it open and having taken a

43

look around the room, her eyes settled on the expensive, cream-colored paper.

Valentina, the murderer! she read, and her inner voice echoed around her mind. *Please, do not reveal ANY details*, she continued reading the red-colored warning. *You will be responsible for the third death. After the first body is found, more information will be provided. Your first mission is to get Jocasta to open up to you. Good luck, player.*

Valentina carefully folded the letter and pushed it back inside its nest.

Who's Jocasta?

Her eyes journeyed the room. Seven women sat in the lounge. *What if she is staff, though?*

Valentina could not help but smile. *Look at me, already in the game. All I wanted was a quiet weekend with my man... I hope names are mentioned because I am in no way in the mood to converse with all these people.*

Her thoughts were interrupted by an irritating ringtone coming from the leather Valentino bag by her side. The redhead that had her back to her swung round and unzipped her bag. Her hands moved around like a hunted mole.

'There you are,' her high-pitched, grating voice announced as her different colored nails pulled out the latest iPhone into the air. 'Who's this now?' she wondered as she continued speaking louder than the booming ringtone. 'Hello? Yes, this is Jocasta. Helen, darling, is that you? I did not recognize the extension. Oh, you're down in logistics. Speak up, dear. I'm on a boat... Yes, left early today to make it... Just a relaxing two-day getaway. Will be back on Monday. Don't say anything as I think I will take sick leave for Monday,' she said, giggling after every sentence. She paced up and down in front of Valentina - in the same manner anyone else would walk in the comfort of their own living room. Jocasta continued her conversation, loudly giving instructions on how to file a certain certificate.

So, you are Jocasta. Just my luck. The most annoying person is the one I am instructed to talk to'

Valentina rolled her eyes and leaned her head on Alexandro's back. Her eyes took one look at the dark sea outside, and her eyelids moved down to offer serenity. Alexandro brought his political conversation to an end and turned to take her into his arms. He kissed the top of her head and leaned back into the tall-back sofa.

Lost in his embrace, Valentina thought that not even Jocasta could ruin her romantic escape to a Greek Island.

Whichever island that may be.

Chapter 7

Ioli parted her ample, coral lips to speak, yet no words came out. The stench that dominated the vast room cloaked her nose, making her mouth essential to breathing. I headed straight to the row of windows to my left. I pulled back heavy, dust-collecting, Roman curtains and stood before the weirdly-shaped glass window. The oval window was separated into two. I opened the lower one with ease and then, with complaints from my joints, I stretched to unlatch the higher, much larger window. Pure country air rushed into the room as Ioli flicked on all the living room lights. Expensive chandeliers came to life, forcing me to momentarily narrow my eyes, offering them time to adjust to the strong light.

Ioli, having guessed right, opened the door to her right. She knelt down and searched the cabinet below the sink. Satisfied with her find, she came out of the guest room toilet with a smirk. She lifted the spray can into the air and soon, the scent of roses masked the miasma that lingered in the skin-piercing, wintry air.

'Sorry,' she said, placing the spray on the floor. 'Since I gave birth, my sense of smell has been off the charts.'

I stood above the late millionaire. 'I see no signs of a struggle. No wounds other than what the rats seem to have done...'

My eyes travelled around his body. His nails and knuckles were clean, his navy blue, checkered robe wasn't ripped, and everything in the room seemed to be in place. 'He is quite old. Could be natural causes...' I mumbled, mostly talking to myself, listing my first thoughts. 'The autopsy will shed some light.'

'Toxicology test, too.'

I looked up at Ioli. 'Tox?'

'Rich people kill in sophisticated ways. Un-messy ways. Poison and so on,' she said and lowered herself to study the old man's bitten face. 'Nasty rodents.'

I rubbed my lower back and straightened my posture. A living room in probably his fifth country home and it occupied more square meters than any house I had ever lived in. Yet, there he was. Dead, bloody, and with empty eye sockets; his eyeballs had become a juicy feast for the rat king and queen. The number of bodies I have seen in my thirty years of doing this ghastly job was likely a three digit number. Though, with every body, my mind always thought of the pointlessness of our short existence. Money, family, love, travel, friendship, a good meal, a good night out. Ephemeral pleasures. Especially now, with the Greek economic crisis making it harder, impossible even, to enjoy the so-called 'good life', I wondered if there was meaning to our lives. Thankfully, these strange thoughts were also ephemeral. Peculiar, worried thoughts that vanished with Tracy's warm hugs, Ioli's laughter and Yiannis' honey-glazed spare ribs.

Suddenly, screeching from what I presumed was a door, echoed to our right. We both looked at each other, and our hands pulled out our guns in silence. Ioli's hand signalled towards the kitchen and gestured to back her up as she checked it out. In stealth mode, we reached the indoor kitchen entrance. We stood each to a side of the door. Ioli placed her hand on the door-knob and looked into my eyes. She mouthed the numbers backwards from three. Footsteps could be heard in the room. Ioli pushed the wooden door back and entered the room with her firearm raised high. 'Freeze! Police!' she shouted in a steady voice. I stood by the door, also with my weapon drawn at eye level, ready to shoot.

The elderly woman with a dirty apron and her hair in a net, unleashed a shrill cry as she jumped back and raised her hands in the air.

'Holy Mary! Please, don't shoot. I... I am... the neighbor. Vasiliki is my name. Oh, dear lord, please, please. You said you are police, right?' she said, her shaking voice slowly descending the decibel scale.

'Yes, you may lower your hands, ma'am,' Ioli said as she lowered her gun.

Mrs. Vasiliki let out a deep sigh and placed her hands on her heart.

'Are you okay?' I asked, having secured my firearm back in its holster.

'I'll be fine. My old eyes have witnessed much in this world. No fright will take out Vasiliki. I tell you that much. May I sit?' she asked, as breathless as a marathon runner, and grabbed a carved, wooden chair before I could reply. I nodded with a smile as she sat down and wiped her forehead. Uneven pieces of parsley and onion were stuck to her calloused, wrinkled hands.

'Let me guess. Meatballs?'

Her bright, blue eyes looked up at me. 'Huh? Oh, yes, yes. My specialty,' she replied, beaming. A proud, Greek cook just like every grandma in this heavenly-made land. 'I was just about to start frying them when I saw the lights over here.'

She paused, unsure of her next words. 'Err, what are you doing here, if I may ask?' Has this got to do with poor Mr. Thanasis' disappearance?'

Ioli cleared her throat and sat down opposite Mrs. Vasiliki.

'When was the last time you saw Mr. Thanasi?'

'Must be over a year now,' she replied, wiping her hands upon her apron.

'And do you always enter without knocking when you see his lights on?' I asked, standing behind Ioli.

Her jaw journeyed downwards and even trembled for a second before she worked up the courage to reply. 'Now, listen here, young man. I am an honest woman and my relationship with Mr, Thanasis is purely platonic...'

'I am not implying otherwise. I am just wondering why you did not knock on the front door.'

'Weird things have been going on and...'

'Weird things?' Ioli asked, anxious to end the old lady's prolonged pause.

'You see, whenever Mr. Thanasis is going to arrive, he sends me a voice message a few days in advance to come and clean the house. Let some fresh air in and bring some groceries. He keeps a key to the kitchen door under that... breast-revealing Aphrodite statue by his cactus garden.'

Again, another long pause. I began to wonder if Mrs. Vasiliki was as my grandma used to say 'all there'. Most of my grandma's friends had problems remembering, yet she remained sharp to the very end of her ninety-two-year-old stay on Earth. This random fact, unfortunately, gave her the 'wrong' right to comment on her friends' well-being.

'Mrs. Vasiliki?' I asked, looking at her fazed-out stare.

'Oh, yes, dear. Where was I? So, a couple of months ago, I hear a car. My house is not near the road,' she said and coughed to clear her dry throat. 'I went to the window, but all I saw was a cloud of dirt drifting along the driveway.'

'Can I get you a glass of water?' Ioli asked, hearing the lady's scratchy voice.

'Oh, no, honey,' she replied, waving her hand to signal no. Gestures and words lived side by side, here in Greece.

'You see, I am not as fast as I used to be,' she continued and rolled her eyes. 'So, I didn't catch the car, but surely someone drove up to the house. I am not your typical nosy, old Greek grandma so I did not come knocking. Even, when the following night I saw a faint light coming from the kitchen. It was only for a minute or two and not the main light. More like a lamp.'

'Were any curtains drawn or any windows open?' I asked, finally sitting down beside Ioli. My knees were working their usual number on me, and I could not decide if they had enough of sitting on the ferry and car or if they had enough of carrying my weight and needed a rest.

Mrs. Vasiliki shook her head. 'Everything was locked and sealed. It was the next morning that I heard down in the village that Mr. Thanasis had gone missing. That is when I decided to come up here. I knocked and peaked in every window, but saw or heard nothing. I did not dare to open the house without his permission. The only reason I opened now was that I was sure someone was here.'

Ioli stopped pinching the top of her fine Greek nose, and her frown died as quickly as it was born. A migraine mixed with over-thinking made quite a ferocious attack on the brain.

'Any lights, sounds, anything since then? It's been weeks...'

'Nothing, until now.'

Ioli turned and looked at me, puzzled; her eyes asking for the next step.

I stood up and thanked Mrs. Vasiliki for all her help. 'Need a ride to your house?' I asked, part kindness, part getting rid of her.

'Oh, no,' she said and giggled. 'The body and brain might be falling apart, yet these feet are my soldiers. Been working these fields since I was twelve years old. I have muscles in my legs you young ones will never have. You and your cross fit, yoga and Paleo diets.'

Laughing a thick, heavy laughter, she placed her wrinkled hands upon the table and lifted herself up. 'As I tell my eight grandkids, nothing will work miracles on your bodies like digging the land,' she continued, ambling to the door. With a wave of her hand, she tottered down the gravelled path, back to her home and her frying.

Ioli pushed back her chair and sprang up. 'I love the proud way grandmothers announce the number of their offspring.'

'If I stood up so fast, I'd probably faint from vertigo or something.'

'Stop acting older than you are, boss,' she said and began to walk back to the nibbled-away body that sat in the living room. 'Why didn't we tell her that he is dead? I mean, she will see the coroner's van and the investigation team. It will all be over the news, too,' she continued, stopping by the arched doorway.

'And leave eight grandkids without meatballs? That would be so un-Greek of me,' I replied with a smile and walked past her. 'I'm going to the car to get my gloves. Can you call HQ? Get the team out here?'

'Sure thing.'

Outside, the temperature had taken a dive. I shivered in the cold breeze and inhaled the fresh air with hints of fireplace wood. Though on the job, I felt peculiarly relaxed, even carefree. Normally, as with the hundreds of cases under my belt, my mind would be drawing out scenarios and theories of what may have happened. Whose car did the neighbor hear? Who benefited from his death? What dark pages from his past are missing? And so on. Now, I was hoping for the most logical explanation of death due to natural causes. What I like to refer to as a simple case. Little did I know, how far more complicated our billionaire's death would come to be.

Chapter 8

Any hopes to guess their destination came to an end with the drowning of the last sun rays. The radiated winter light was swallowed by the Greek sea, and gloom devoured the ferry. The lingering clouds in the night sky occluded the star-light and diminished Apollo's hopes of guessing the island.

'If I could see the stars, I would navigate my way around. My father, a fisherman, taught me everything about the stars. No need for compasses back in the day.'

'I'm pretty sure we are heading East,' Maximos, the jean-wearing farmer, said while scratching his index nail.

'There are more directions than just the plain four taught in school,' Diana commented, placing her right leg upon her bare left; her dress stopping only an inch before revealing more than just flesh. Noticing Maximos's curious gaze, she put away her mirror and turned to his direction. 'I mean, we could be heading North East or South East, and God knows at what angle or degrees or whatever they call it.'

'Now, there's who knows our destination. God,' Bishop Arsenios said and shook his wife's knee with his huge hand. Her petite figure shook from head to toe and she forced a flat smile; her eyes remained expressionless, though Valentina was sure that

Salome checked to see if her mountain of a husband had his eyes on the provocative, sexy, cliché-blonde, bright-red-lipstick wearing lady. Diana was no young dove, but hid her real age well by drawing attention to her 'other assets'.

Valentina concluded that their destination was not a mystery for her mind to get wound up about. Her inner mind mechanisms were laid to rest by Alexandro's rough hands that were caressing her hair; naughty fingers escaping their task and playing with her ear lobe. With her head upon his leg, she felt every wild wave that the ferry conquered as it sliced into the sea, destination unknown. Her beady eyes took a voyage around the ship's ceiling. It was flawless. Valentina, as a true islander, had seen her fair share of boats. All with signs of time's attack and the mighty sun's invasion. There were no spider-web cracks in the paint to be seen.

Could this be the ferry's maiden journey? she thought and pondered about how much money was put into the new mysterious venture, *I'd hate to receive a price tag at the end of all this.*

The rest of their large group was the focus of Alexandro's eyes. The upper-class group, busy reading their envelopes and getting to know each other intrigued him. Born and raised by a family of limited means –he hated the word poor- Alexandro began work in the police force just as the crisis hatched out of Pandora's egg and unleashed its evils upon the once-proud nation of Greece. He never saw a pay rise; only cuts. His first salary was the largest he received, and it all went downhill from there. A river running down a steep slope, dragging Alexandro's hopes of a better life and flooding his chances of living an unworried –money-wise at least- life. Just like the majority of young, passionate Greeks with a job, he envied those he presumed were *better-off* than him.

Maximos excluded, the people standing before him easily fell into his 'jealous list'. Brand clothes, expensive jewelry, a posh manner of speaking, cell phones that cost twice his monthly wage - he noticed it all. Most of all, his inner green monster despised the group of three siblings that sat carefree in the corner to his right. The two brothers were showing their introverted sister an array of humorous videos on their phones causing tumultuous laughter to escape her pearly teeth. Alexandro felt and knew well that these thoughts of his were, simply put, wrong. Thus, he never shared them with Valentina. He needed no lecture about how he should cherish everything he had, - love, food, a roof over his head. How he made ends meet compared to millions of unemployed compatriots. He knew all this. Yet, these three rich kids caused an eruption of thoughts and daydreams about winning the lottery or having been born into a billionaire's home.

Suddenly, all thoughts were interrupted as conversations died instantly and voices turned into short-lived shrieks. All light vanished at once, leaving them in darkness.

'Ladies and gentlemen, please direct your attention to the marvelous island of...'

Eyes turned to the direction of the speakers, eagerly awaiting Platonas' next word.

'... Hotel Murder!'

'Wait. What?' the slim gentleman in the navy blue suit said, rising from his seat. Eugene had spent the entire journey with his nose buried in his novel, yet anticipating greatly on the revelation of the island. A real ladies' man, the mystery weekend left him indifferent. He accepted the invitation with the only goal of adding to his 'subjugation list.' Women were a mere sexual object to him. As a political campaign manager who wrote speeches for successful members of parliament, Eugene always had the right words to lure women to his bachelor's den. In combination with his smooth voice and manly, handsome facial features, Eugene's list was now in the hundreds. Disappointment hit him hard when he realized his options. Ladies over fifty, a girl with her brothers, others with their men and not a single 'looker' among the staff. *The island will be loaded with pussy*, was his comforting thought. So, he ducked down to page 243 of Life Of Pi and waited to hear the town of *lucky ladies*.

His displeasure grew upon hearing the conversation beside him.

'Well, what do you see?' Hope asked. 'Is it Mykonos?'

Galatea giggled and stroked her blind friend's cold cheek. 'You wish! All I can see is a rock in the sea with lights on a wooden pier.'

'A rock?'

'Hope, it doesn't look bigger than a few acres. I cannot see any buildings on it, that's for sure...'

'Me neither,' her blind friend interrupted her, bringing a warm smile upon Galatea's face. Their friendship began when their ages were a single digit, and Galatea had taken a while to reach a point of enjoying Hope's witty remarks- as sarcastic, self-mocking, sexist, racist, or blasphemous as they sometimes were.

'A dark piece of land? That's it?' Jocasta asked, standing up and staring outwards. Taller than the rest, she spoke without looking at anyone in particular. Her eyes remained focused ahead; only when on the phone, did her head bobble up and down as she waved her hands, pacing around like a hound dog in search of a rabbit hole and mysteriously avoiding getting tangled up in the wires escaping her flashy-covered phone. Valentina loathed people who –while not driving- spoke on a hands-free headset. *Just stick the damn thing to your ear, woman.*

Alexandro's voice captured her attention away from Jocasta. 'Wait, look,' he said and pointed out the window. Valentina was not sure if 'window' was the right term for the cavity on the side of the ferry. She would have to look it up, later. *I hope they have WiFi,* she thought. Yes, it was a romantic weekend away, but after love making, Alexandro took either of two paths. Hefty sleep or lousy, trashy TV. Valentina took the same course of action either way. She snuggled up to his warm body and scrolled through her favorite sites of weird and fascinating articles from around the world.

Why do large women enjoy sex more?

Thirty ways to use your old milk bottles around the house.

Famous singer caught with a hooker in a parking lot.

Anaconda in the Amazon committed suicide by swallowing itself.

Make your monsters obey! Tips for young parents.

Hours could sway by, and in the darkness of the bedroom, her cell's light shone brightly upon her face. Alexandro's snoring – heavy breathing, according to him- would echo around the room, reminding her of the dawn approaching and another day at work, where she would zombie around, due to a lack of healthy sleep.

Valentina felt the boat tilt slightly below her feet as she stood up and approached Alexandro. The ferry turned and their view changed. A dazzlingly lit pier broke the black panorama before them. A firefly alone in the dark. All guests stood in silence, their eyes on the dock with red carpet unfolded upon it; a teasing, red tongue inviting them into the mouth of the small island. The engines quietened down, and the ferry relaxed, drifting to dock.

Just then, two bangs were heard from above, and fireworks colored the sky. Suddenly, more lights came to life, revealing a road heading uphill. A second wave of light divulged a three-story mansion occupying the flat top of the little, lone hill.

Though brand new –or perhaps newly renovated- the building gave out a medieval, gothic vibe. Monstrous gargoyles were strategically placed above lights giving them an unworldly feel, the front door resembled that of a castle from eras long past, and iron bars stood solidly in front of the tongue-shaped windows. Cracks were painted upon the grey, rock-like bricks and Poison Ivies were placed and spread around the walls. Both with a mission to give the mansion an 'old feel' to it.

'Someone has seen way too many gothic movies,' Valentina whispered in Alexandro's ear as she hugged him from behind, her hands meeting above his belly button.

The side of the ferry bumped against black tires hanging from the long pier, and the crew immediately began unloading the boat, beginning with guests' suitcases. Platonas appeared with his widest smile and invited the group of holiday winners to follow him.

He rushed ahead, avoiding questions shot at him and raised his hands in a grand gesture. 'This way; your mystery awaits!'

It was a short walk, and the hill did not boast a greatly uphill road. Neither fact thwarted the upper-class members of the group from moaning about having to make the journey from the dock to the hotel.

'Great. A march,' the tall man said to the banker next to him.

'Indeed. Neofytos,' the banker said, extending his hand.

'Dr. Loucas Michael,' he replied.

'What kind of doctor?'

'Dentist.'

'Hmm,' Neofytos replied, unimpressed. Since a child, he had loathed dentists. Not as much as clowns. But he still despised them.

Meters from the entrance Platonas stopped, his eyes sparkling with excitement and his face unable to hide his joy. The rest of the employees were joyful as well. They wished for nothing to go wrong. In an age of raging unemployment, they had found a job with a four-figure pay.

Music from the Lord of the Rings soundtrack boomed through the night air, and more lights came to life around the gigantic entry door. Smoke sneaked out as the wooden castle-like door was lowered, and a dark figure of a man was revealed.

'Ladies and gentlemen, I present to you, your host, the owner of Hotel Murder, Aristoteli Minoa.'

'Are we supposed to clap?' Hope joked into Galatea's ear and gave her a nudge as they stopped behind Platonas. Both ladies proved fitter than their younger counterparts and led the group uphill.

All eyes were set on the mysterious man stepping out through the smoke. A tall man for a Greek, dressed for the ball with black reading glasses on his Roman nose. His nonchalant gaze and calm, warm, inviting smile were the first features to draw Valentina's interest as she scanned the forty-something, Herculean built man.

His shaved bald head glowed from the surrounding strong lights as he ambled towards them with arms wide open.

'My dear guests, welcome to my hotel. May all your mysterious dreams and secret desires come true...'

'Great. A long speech. My tummy is begging to be fed,' Alexandro whispered –as much as he was capable of whispering.

'Don't worry. I will not bore you or leave you standing here. Come in, my friends...'

'Did he hear me?' Alexandro asked, seeking an answer from his bedazzled girlfriend. He highly doubted it. Aristoteli Minoa stood meters away, and the medieval music was still playing. Lowered volume, but still on-going. 'Valentina?'

'Huh? No, of course not. Handsome man, right?'

Valentina turned towards him. 'Right?'

A frown appeared upon his face as he asked her if she truly was expecting an answer.

'Why not? You show me girls all the time when we are out...'

'Yeah, to notice how slutty they are or to discuss...'

'Same shit,' she replied and laid a kiss upon his dry lips.

'...come in! The staff will show you to your rooms. Snacks and drinks are provided there, yet save your appetite for tonight's feast.' Aristoteli Minoa continued.

Like wary sheep, the group moved together into the grand belly of the fortress. Amazement spread as guests saw the luxurious, yet peculiar inside.

It was a grand hall, to say the least. Magnificent works of art hung from its magnolia-painted walls, elegant Greek statues were placed around the vast room, and shiny, gold-plated chandeliers shone from above. A large, round mahogany table dominated the center of the room, glowing, showing off how perfectly varnished it was. Free of dirty fingerprints, it hosted a row of porcelain elephants and a tall, twisted candle holder with three lit, white, aromatic candles. Yet, among the opulent ornaments, hints of the hotel's true nature could be easily spotted. A fake dagger dipped into a red candle, life-sized murder weapons from Cluedo lined up on a shelf to their left, a headless statue, a toy snake wrapped around the legs of another, portraits depicting crime scenes from Jack the Ripper and the shape of a body made out of tape just below the grand staircase to their right.

Clio, the only girl in the Afroudaki triplet squad, stood a few feet behind the rest. Her brother, Elias, turned to notice her shiver. Her hand stroked the back of her neck.

'What's wrong?'

'Spider sense.'

Just the words made him come closer.

Spider sense was an inside joke in their home. Yet, nothing was ever funny about it. Clio, ever since she was a child, sensed a weird tingling on the back of her neck whenever something bad was about to happen. Her brothers referred to it as her spider sense. She hated the term as spiders topped her list of creepy, disgusting beings. At first, her parents thought it was cute, labelled it as a coincidence, and then learned to trust it. Clio had felt this way, just before their grandma's death, their uncle's car crash and even the earthquake of 2008.

'What's up?' their brother, Dinos, asked.

'Spider sense.'

Dinos burst out laughing. 'It's Hotel Murder! Of course, someone is about to die!'

Chapter 9

Holidays. A craved-after word.

In a world of working daily, the majority of people in stressful, tiring professions, everyone desires a break. Away from responsibilities, the office, the kids, the boss, the chores, and the cooking. Away from the soul-piercing daily routine.

Maybe this fact is what gives the magical aura to the days away.

A better version of yourself comes to life. Calmer, happier, nicer, more flexible and more negotiable. As if matters that seemed troubling before, fade away to an oblivion of vacation bliss. A different schedule, a different view, a different you.

With her eye peeping through the slightly open bathroom door, Valentina grinned at a fully-clothed Alexandro passed out on the king-sized bed. Valentina sat down on the toilet and took her phone into her hands. *Strong WiFi! I'm starting to like this hotel.*

Twenty minutes later, she unglued her eyes from the screen, stood up and shed her clothing. The growling from the room was no mystery to be solved. Alexandro was snoring, his mind lost far away in dreamland.

'A shower without a time limit. Manna from heaven.'

The hot, steamy water fell upon her skin as she opened the first miniature bottle, labelled imperial shower gel. The perfumed scent, redolent of spring, overwhelmed her senses.

Having lost track of time, Valentina stepped out of the shower and opted to remain naked. She pulled back the bathroom door, letting enclosed steam escape the room.

'Well, look who has decided to finally step out of the shower,' Alexandro complained without turning to face her. He lay on the bed, awake with eyes shut. 'We have to be down soon, and I was thinking of showering, too.'

Valentina's right corner of her mouth moved upwards. 'I guess then that we don't have time for sex. Better rush and get ready.'

Both of his eyelids sprinted open, and Alexandro sat up, upon the king sized bed. He licked his lips and said 'No, no. We have all the time in the world. I think dinner is like nine-ish...'

'Men!' Valentina laughed, shook her head and approached the bed.

Alexandro crawled to the edge of the bed and grabbed her by the waist as she walked by. He twirled her around and fell upon her unclothed, smooth, alluring body.

'I think you are way too dressed for the occasion, mister.'

She loved the way he hastily undressed, pulling clothes off the top of his head and kicking away others. Most of all, she was smitten by the boyish grin that crowned his chiselled face as he stood naked before her. Her hand reached out and took his erection into her hand causing him to shiver and leaned down to kiss her. Valentina placed her hands upon his back, and her nails travelled back and forth, before journeying into his thick, rich hair. Alexandro bit on her ear lobe and entered her slowly. His large hands settled to her sides as he lifted himself up and pushed further in.

Two bodies intertwined. She was a blossoming, Persian jasmine and he was her supporting wall. Valentina had no former lovers, yet was sure she would never feel this way with any other man. Her eruption came in waves and with a wide smile on her flushed face, she bit his bottom lip tenderly.

As Valentina dived into euphoria, the rest of the guests were busy dressing up for the evening. Gowns, expensive dresses, tuxedos, suits, flashy jewelry. All came out to play.

Soon, pungent, tantalizing aromas floated out of the grand dining room and conquered the air, calling the guests down. Members of the staff waited for them as the guests came down the carpeted, marble stairs. They held silver platters, some with tuna canapés, and some with tall wine glasses filled with bubbly champagne. Two by two, the guests descended the twisted in a perfect spiral staircase and exchanges of 'good evenings' were heard. Gossiping was exchanged in whispering voices and limited to each duo.

Valentina and Alexandro were last to arrive, though, just in time as Platonas announced that dinner was served.

Fine dinnerware lay upon the long table. Aristoteli stood at the head of the table, welcoming the guests into the high-ceilinged room. Golden, church-like chandeliers hung from above and brightly threw light around the vast room.

Dinner was served 'Greek meze' style. First came the little plates with the various dips, closely followed by hot pita bread and village salad. A variety of meats and grilled vegetables came next, and once devoured were replaced with more.

'Holy crap, Robin. My utility belt is about to explode!'

'So, I'm guessing you're Batman?' Valentina replied, rolling her eyes. 'How you ever had so *many* girlfriends, I wonder. Comic book flirting and all.'

Alexandro's grin spread across his face. 'I always laugh how you stress the word many. But seriously, I cannot believe we are eating all of this free of charge.'

Alexandro's delight only grew, when an array of desserts was soon presented.

'Well, well, well. Jackpot. There's even galatoboureko! Heaven, baby, heaven.'

Valentina opted for a freshly-cut apple and watched as her man got lost in ecstasy, surrounded by three pieces of honey-dripping galatoboureko. As she lifted her tissue to wipe Alexandro's chin, Aristoteli announced that the night was young and asked to be followed into the next room - the ballroom, as he called it.

Traditional music boomed out of the four over-hanging speakers, and Aristoteli led the way to the dance floor.

'Good way to get us out of the way for the help to clean up,' Hope commented, as she walked hand-in-hand with Galatea, who was describing the room to her.

'Same chandeliers, yet the ceiling is not as high. You would love it. The curtains...'

Behind them, Diana walked close by and having had a look at her white-gold watch with the diamond numbers, she yelled with excitement and leaped beside Aristoteli, her arms opened wide, ready to dance.

Her glittery red heels gracefully travelled around the dance floor as Diana had apparently not only maintained the body of a twenty year old for the last three decades, she had also preserved her wild teen side when it came to partying.

Valentina and Alexandro lingered by the wooden, tall bar enjoying the free alcohol. The boy behind the bar had left his post, having been called down to the kitchen for an emergency, as he referred to it. As he exited, he apologized and uttered the short sentence that brought bliss to the guest. 'Feel at home, take whatever you want. I'll be right back...'

Alexandro stirred his whiskey, one eye on the swirling ice cubes, the other on Diana's dancing figure.

'She's got quite a body, huh?'

'You miss nothing,' he replied, now with both eyes on Valentina's.

'Nope,' she smiled. 'I also noticed how she keeps checking the time on her Rolex and how there is no personnel to be seen and...'

Alexandro leaned forward and smelled her neck. He took in a deep breath and delicately kissed her neck, bringing her words to a full stop. 'Officer, you are over thinking again.'

'I thought we were here to solve the mystery.'

'We are. As soon as we have another free drink and hit the dance floor.'

Valentina laughed out loud. She enjoyed seeing him relax for a change. She missed the carefree man that her heart had fallen for. Now, with every pay cut and every new tax, she witnessed the stress surround and overwhelm him. He worried about the rent, the bills, and how they would manage to raise children in this sinking ship of a country.

Valentina poured herself another glass of fine, crisp, white wine. Her prize for a superb getaway from the world. The drinks came and perished on their thirsty lips, yet their dance never came. Diana, having first walked to the door and taken a peak outside, marched over to the stereo system and abruptly switched the music off. All heads in the room turned her direction.

Just as every bad actress out there, she dramatically swallowed a deep breath and spoke loudly as she made her announcement.

'Fellow guests, tragedy has hit us. As we partied, a murder has taken place. Right under our noses. Quick, everyone to the stairwell. The body is still fresh.'

Diana exhaled; her smile revealing her joy of remembering her lines.

Never before was a corpse approached by such an ebullient group. Maximos led the group and pushed open the heavy ballroom doors.

'Oh my!' Jocasta said as the group came to a pause a few feet away from the tangled body.

'Boy, does that blood look real,' Eugene added.

'Isn't that the doctor?' the bishop asked his wife.

'Was he a guest or an actor?' she replied.

'What's with all the envelopes?' Clio asked her brothers.

Only Valentina and Alexandro remained silent and confused. They held hands and exchanged worried, concerned looks.

'What are we supposed to do now? Who has the next clue? Diana?' Apollo spoke up.

'My task was to get you all out here. That's it,' she replied.

Silence fell upon them; only Galatea's whispering could be heard as she described the scene to Hope.

'It's Dr. Loucas Michael. The tall doctor with the flashy teeth, I told you about. His body seems to have been thrown down the stairs. His limbs are bent and stretched out in a funny way. If you get what I mean. There is a large pool of blood, in which he lays. There are numerous small envelopes floating in the blood, but nothing appears to be written on them.'

'Well, we can't just stand here. Maybe, we are supposed to look around for clues?' Theodore, the congressman, suggested.

'Why don't we just ask the good, old doctor eh?' Maximos said with an upbeat, mocking fake laugh. 'Yo, Doc. How did you die?' he continued as he knelt by the body. 'Well, I say. Damn good actor, he is.'

Maximos was ready to poke him when Valentina cried 'Stop!'

There was something in her cry that made everyone turn to see her.

'I... I... Don't think he is pretending.'

The words took a few seconds to settle and make nests in brains around the room. Eyes ping-ponged from the corpse to Valentina's ashen face. Only Dinos and Elia had their eyes focused on their sister, Clio. Her premonition was coming true in a short amount of time.

'Are those your lines, dear?' Hope asked, speaking up, her weak voice struggling to be heard.

'It's probably a dummy. Talking about lines, mine are to advise you all to return to the ballroom and I will call the police,' Apollo said, stepping forward. 'I'm sure actors will appear soon as detectives or something.'

'Shut up! All of you just shut up,' Alexandro said. 'Step away from the body. Now! The real police are already here.'

Alexandro took his time to accept the fact that the body before him was real. No make-up artist could make it look so real. No theatre blood came close to the fluid unleashed from the doctor's veins.

'Please gather by the entrance and remain still and relaxed,' Valentina added and joined Alexandro, who had knelt by the body and was checking for vital signs. 'He's dead, for sure,' he whispered to her as she stood by his side.

'Shouldn't we call for a member of staff? I mean, we can't call it in. We have no freaking idea where the hell we are.'

'Where's Aristoteli? The owner was feasting with us.'

'He sneaked out over half an hour ago. I didn't think much of it, then. He never came back,' Valentina replied, pulling back her blonde hair and locking it in a high ponytail. It was time to examine the body. 'The blood can't be from the fall. It's too much. Can you see any entry wounds?'

Alexandro shook his head and decided to lift the doctor by his left shoulder. Both were faced with a chest covered in stab wounds.

Meanwhile, away from the body, the guests discussed their own theories about the unexplained turn of events unfolding before them.

'Told you those two were actors,' Diana said, taking another sip of champagne.

'Yes, you did, dear,' Galatea agreed, nodding her head to the point her thin-framed glasses slid down her nose.

'How did you guess?' Hope asked, her hand never leaving Galatea's.

'Well, can't you see the difference? Not our class,' Diana stated her theory and then widened her eyes. 'Oh, sorry, babes. I did not think. It's just a matter of speech, you know? I'm not daft. I know you can't see...'

Hope could not contain her laughter. 'No offense taken, Diana. But, are we sure?'

'Yes, I'm sure. They are just trying to scare us.'

Clio remained between her two brothers, her long fingers running along her iPhone's screen. 'I'm calling mum,' she said and lifted the phone to her ear.

Neofytos, the strict-looking banker, placed a cigar between his thin lips and announced that he was heading outside for a smoke. More of an invitation than an announcement, he looked around in search for fellow smokers.

'Good idea. I need a cigarette and some cold air,' Eugene said and walked towards him.

'Hasn't mum picked up yet?' Elia asked his sister.

'I can't seem to get through. There's no signal. That's weird. It had full reception before.'

Neofytos pulled down the door handle a few times before swearing that the door was locked.

'Can they just lock us in? That's absurd,' Apollo said. 'I think we need to get that owner out here or find Platonas. He seemed to be the only one from the staff that was entitled to reveal details to us.'

'Ask the two actors by the body,' Diana said.

Valentina stood up and turned towards them. 'We aren't actors. We are police officers and, ma'am, not to panic you, but this is a real dead body.'

'Okay, fuck this shit, I'm getting out of here,' Jocasta said and approached the nearest window.

Suddenly, all lights went out, and darkness fell upon them. A loud rumbling noise emerged from all around them. Heavy, steel planks descended and covered each window; the darkness turning into pitch black.

Screams and cries floated in the air and hands reached out to find someone to hold.

'They are sealing us in!' Salome, the bishop's wife, yelled and leaned into her stout husband.

'I'm sure it is just part of the game, dear. Try to relax. You know how you can get.'

Most followed Clio's idea for light and raised their cell phones into the air.

'Is anyone getting any reception?' Alexandro asked.

'Nope.'

'Me neither!'

'How can they kill our phones? How is that even possible?' Hope wondered.

'It's easier than you think,' Dinos said and tightened his hug around his ashen-faced sister.

As swiftly as it had vanished, the light came back to the room. Every single light bulb came back to life, revealing the sealed-off windows. Maximos banged against the steel and whistled in amazement.

'Now, what?'

Chapter 10

'If someone came to the house, either to see him or kill him, that means the old man told that certain someone about his plan to go to his forgotten cottage in Rhodes. We checked all his appointments, office and home phone calls, and whereabouts, dating back days to his disappearance...' Ioli said and paused as she stepped off the ferry; our feet back on the ground in Athens. 'Am I making sense or am I rambling? Those nasty waves shook my brains to scrambled grey cells.'

Scratching my neck, I replied that I was following her drift. 'Go on,' I urged her.

'Well, we know exactly who he talked to those days as his bodyguard, chauffeur, wife, and secretary were always with him. I mean one or the either... God, that sea really messed up my vocabulary... Anyway, the old neighbor said he sent her a voice message. His cell was with a private company, if I recall correctly. They just sent us his phone call list to help with investigations, and printouts of his message inbox after we got a warrant.'

I walked beside her up to the police car that waited for us by the quiet bar that served the pack of sea dogs that roamed the old harbor. A rookie sat in the driver's seat, putting in an effort to look professional and making sure we did not catch his young eyes scanning the two 'working girls' that stood behind the bar's premises, close to the men's lavatories.

'So, what you are saying is we head out to the phone company and check his voice box? If they save them, that is.'

'Nowadays, they save everything,' she replied and opened the car's rear left door. I walked round the car and sat shotgun. 'Brrr, cold winds today, huh?' I asked and looked at his name tag. 'So, Tito, do you know where QV2's main offices are?'

He blinked rapidly and moved his lips, yet no words came out at first. 'I thought we were going back to headquarters. I'm sorry, sir, no one informed me of our route...'

'Calm down, boy. It's a last-second decision. So?'

'So...?'

'Here,' Ioli interrupted and handed him her phone. The map and route were ready on the screen. 'And quick,' she added.

Twenty minutes later, we arrived outside of the twelve-story glass building that housed the telecommunications company. A flashing, signature blue sign dominated the entrance. 'QV2 welcomes you,' the electric sliding doors announced as we entered the luxurious office building.

We bee-lined to the enormous front desk where a plus-size girl, in her mid-twenties, wearing a tight, white shirt and an overly-happy-for-such-a-late-hour expression welcomed us to QV2. She then pushed a button on the desk in front of her and lowered her head microphone to mouth level.

'Mrs. Pandora, the police are here... Yes, I will send them right up,' she said and pushed the flashing, green button again. It turned red for a second and then faded back to a dull grey. 'Mrs. Pandora will see you right now. Third floor, turn right, office 306,' she said, maintaining the same merry tone.

'Imagine that voice on a Monday morning after a Sunday shift,' Ioli said and shivered as the elevator doors met in front of us.

'Third floor,' *Mrs. Elevator* soon announced and the doors departed from their embrace. We stepped out, and with the cheery voice in our heads, we followed instructions and headed right down the long hallway; our eyes scanned the metallic plated numbers upon the doors.

'300... 302... 304... here we are,' Ioli said as she mumbled along the way.

I knocked on the cherry-red door and waited for a reply.

'Come in.' The steady voice came from inside. I pictured a strict-looking fifty-year-old with a tight suit on, yet my cliché image could not have been further from the truth. A tall woman, in her late thirties with silky, olive skin and lively eyes stood behind her mahogany desk with her hand extended to the two armchairs in front of her. She wore a pair of faded jeans, those with multiple rips along the sides. Her belly was on display as her bright, yellow tank top failed to cover it. Though a tall lady, her feet were carried by black high heels.

'How may I be of assistance, officers?' she asked as her eyes watched us settle in the white armchairs she had motioned to. Patterns of red raindrops decorated the white leather, while the armchair's twisted wooden legs caught my attention. At least, they were more comfortable than they looked.

'It's about the case of Thanasis Zampetides...' Ioli began to say.

'Yes, we have already provided everything to investigators...'

'After a court order was presented,' Ioli replied. She hated people interrupting her.

'Company policy,' Mrs. Pandora said and sat down in her chair.

'I am Captain Costa Papacosta, and this is Lieutenant Ioli Cara,' I said before Ioli could reply. 'We are investigating a different aspect, a new idea based on new evidence. Is there any chance you have backups of voice messages?'

Mrs. Pandora tapped her well-shaped, manicured nails upon the desk's surface. Her new-born frown curved her thin, arched eyebrows into a McDonald's sign. 'Yes, we can retrieve voice messages. Our servers keep backups dating two years back. Then, the system begins to erase them by day. However, Captain Papacosta, your court order was pretty specific. Phone calls, messages, emails. Voice messages were not mentioned, and we require written permission from an individual to release his voice messages. Or a specific court order, of course.'

Ioli's annoyance did not take long to come to life. 'Well, *we* need them. Our individual is dead, you see, and will not be giving his written permission. Waiting for a court order will take days. Days in which his killer will escape. Do you wish us to inform his family and let your wealthiest clients know, how you aided his murderer in his escape? Now, that's a box you should not open, Mrs. Pandora,' Ioli said, leaning slightly forward. Her fingers interlocked, and her arms rested upon her legs as she spoke.

Mrs. Pandora locked her eyes upon Ioli's. 'Listen, I'm not trying to be a bitch...'

I could almost hear Ioli's thoughts. *Well, you're doing a fine job at being one.*

'... I really do want to help. You have to understand, I answer to a lot of people above me. Anyway, you're in luck. First, it's the weekend, and none of them are present at such an hour and second, my husband - AKA top-notch, tech geek - is in his office as we always work the same hours. He should be able to provide you with everything you need. Though, please, put forward the procedures for a court order. If your case goes to court and you present Mr. Zampetides' voice messages as evidence, my husband and I will get into trouble with our bosses. I will aid you now to help with your case, but please have the paperwork sent to me ASAP.'

Ioli smiled and stood up, extending her ring-wearing hand for a shake. 'Not a bitch, after all,' she joked.

'Tell my husband that when we go up to the labs,' Mrs. Pandora replied and slid her hand into Ioli's.

Five minutes later and the elevator informed us that we had stopped on the eleventh floor. Soon, we stood in a long hallway with a glass wall on one side. Machinery and computers filled our horizon. A handsome, goofy-looking man dressed in a white lab coat stood by an open glass door. 'Hey, babe,' his first two words came out as his eyes lit up at the sight of his wife.

'Newlyweds,' I whispered.

Their fingers met, and he fought back the urge to kiss her. She explained our story to him, and we watched as he rubbed his strong chin and grunted a couple of long 'hmms'. Finally, he lifted his reading glasses into his thick, curly hair and asked us to follow him.

'I never knew wires came in so many colors,' Ioli commented, keeping her voice down, as we followed him into the futuristic room.

A low buzzing sound escorted us through a maze of machines. A background pulled out of a science fiction film. The cheap, B-movie kind that I enjoyed as a teen. A few more 'lab rats' passed by us, their heads bowed and their eyes glued to their notes. None were paying much attention to our presence.

We were formally introduced to Themis as he led us to a room that resembled a conference room more than an office. He sat behind a gigantic screen, and his fingers clicked away. 'Thanasis Zampetides, you said, right?' he mumbled and continued clicking; his expert fingers resembling those of a professional pianist, running along the different keys.

'Okay, I'm in,' he announced. 'Voice messages... hmm... Okay... Got any specific dates?'

'Try the last week of September and run through the days until the 1st of December, the day he was reported missing,' Ioli said.

Themis continued playing his new-age symphony; the data on the screen was reflected in his round specs. He scrolled through the intel' and announced, 'Thirty-two voice messages. Wow, the old man used them a lot. In the age of Viber, WhatsApp, Messenger and so on, we don't see many clients with such high numbers.'

'It seemed to be his preference,' I commented. 'Can you exclude, for now, those received and sent by known numbers? I mean, people from his contact list?' I added.

'Of course,' he replied. 'Only one message sent to an unknown number.

'Can we hear it?' Ioli asked, placing her hand on the desk.

Our expert did not reply. Instead, his hand landed on the flashy red mouse and he clicked on PLAY.

'This is Thanasis Zampetakis. I do not take kindly to receiving threatening letters. Blackmailing is a serious crime. I know you feel with the evidence you hold against me that you have me in your hand, however, I do urge you to think twice. Prison sentences are tough to cope with. I will be at your meeting point. I will come alone as ordered. Do not contact me again.'

The old man sounded firm, yet with a second listen, you could almost hear the desperation and worry in his voice.

'Can we get information from the number he sent the message to?'

'Let me check,' he replied, and his hovering hands attacked the keyboard yet again.

'Nope. No details. It's a card-phone number. Sold in every kiosk, on every corner.'

'Shit,' Ioli said and ran her hands through her black hair. 'Can we at least trace the number? I saw a film once, and they pinpointed a phone to the nearest tower...'

'The number has been deactivated. You see here...' he said and pointed to a red light in the corner of the screen. Ioli was ready to curse again, when Themis continued, giving us a touch of hope. '...I could tell you the exact point the phone was when it received the message, though. Give me a moment or two.'

As he clicked away, his proud wife's hand settled upon his shoulder, rubbing it gently. Ioli and I remained silent, eager for a clue to latch onto.

Chapter 11

'Come on, Mum. It's starting soon!'

'Finish your vegetables, and then you can be excused,' Pavlo's mother replied to her impatient son. Not that she blamed him. She, too, wanted nothing more than to go to the living room and tune in to the adventurous event, but she was a mother, and her offspring's well-being came before entertainment.

The clocks around Greece struck nine and people were ready for the final episode of Survivor. The hit show had returned a few months ago to their TV sets and had become the biggest thing in years. Countless hours were spent discussing the players, the games and of course, the voting. And tonight, it was all coming to an end. The grand finale was just minutes away.

Snack-covered coffee tables welcomed their respective families and groups of friends, and everyone smiled in excitement as the evening news came to an end.

Rival channels stayed out of the path of the juggernaut show, offering a variety of repeats and indifferent programming, with many so-called anti-Survivor fans opting for a night out.

The music that accompanied the opening credits escaped from open windows as the majority of TVs played the show. Certain bars and cafes were even having Survivor-themed nights.

I was just about to settle down my rather large behind and take Tracy into a hug when, yet again, she remembered another *essential* item missing from our pizza-infested table. 'Costa, dear. The ketchup? Oh, and some napkins, babe.'

I contained my tongue and replied with a short-lived, flat smile. *Happy wife= happy life.*

I sat down just in time for the recap. 'Previously on Survivor...'

Those were the only three words any one of us heard of the show. Suddenly, the TV screen switched to black. People at public events were the first to begin shouting. At home, hands reached out for remote controls, while others checked the wiring. Strangely enough, all other stations were broadcasting fine.

A flashy, silver cycle appeared on our screens. Soon, a crimson-colored number ten took shape, and the countdown began.

Lips counted with the bloody-looking numbers and minds processed the anxiety regarding what the producers of Survivor had come up with.

Little did anyone know of the panic at the Sky channel. Their signal was interrupted abruptly, and their sensational, triumphant show had vanished from the air. Executives cursed in all directions, and tech-geeks desperately searched for a solution.

'Who the hell is hijacking us?' a producer yelled.

'Where is the signal coming from? Can they just broadcast from our signal like that?' a petite brunette executive dressed in a tight brown dress asked, wandering up to the control room.

Many questions were raised; no answers were provided.

Silence fell upon all as the numbers reached zero and light came back to our screens. All eyes witnessed a vast room with a group of people looking around, stress and worry clear upon their faces.

I stood up at once. 'That's Valentina and Alexandro!'

'My God, you're right. What is this?' Tracy said, leaning forward, departing from the comfortable back of the leather sofa.

'My fellow Greeks...' a robotic voice boomed over the live image of people searching for a way out of the room. The group of people all came to a pause, stopping to listen to the mechanical voice as well.

'...it has been eight years since our economy collapsed. Eight years of suffering for mistakes not made by the common people. We are governed by dogs. Dogs obedient to the World Bank and our new oppressors, the EU and its banks, led by Angela Merkel. We have seen our children's rations shrivel up because of worthless politicians and greedy bankers. New measures have just been announced and we, like sheep, sit down to watch Survivor. The real survivor is our everyday lives. The homeless are the ones truly without food. But, no more. I have gathered a select group of people, each representing a larger group of vampires with their fangs deep into our necks.'

Our screens went blank once again, only to come back with a dead body on display. Pavlo's mother gasped and covered her son's innocent eyes.

'This is Dr. Loucas Michael. Our first victim of the evening,' the robotic, deep, distorted voice continued. 'A doctor at Evangelismos Hospital. A public hospital. His wages were coming from taxpayers. From all of us. Like many, he took advantage of his position and took money on the side. Money to bump you up on surgery lists, to get on transplant lists, to get you better medication. Money from hard-earned wages and pensions. The money being passed around in envelopes in our hospitals needs to stop.'

The camera zoomed onto the brown envelopes soaking up the doctor's blood. A time of two hours appeared in the corner and began travelling backwards.

'The Minister of Health has two hours to announce the firing of the list of doctors he has just received on his fax. All guilty. Guilty of the same crimes of Dr. Loucas Michael. Also, to announce the placement of non-government, private sector controllers in hospital boards. If he fails to do so, the next victim will be chosen, and his or her blood will be on the Minister's hands.'

The screen darkened, and photos of faces flew around the screen. 'Let's meet our players. Each guilty. Each with filthy hands. You, the viewer will choose our next victim. Use the hashtag #*nexttodie* and the name you wish to punish.'

A photo of a blonde lady appeared. 'Diana Alexopoulou. Owner of Humbo. The country's largest chain of supermarkets and toy stores. During the last five years, her net worth has risen to two hundred and thirty million, while all employees at Humbo were forced to take a twenty percent pay cut and new employees were illegally forced to sign contracts accepting ten-hour shifts. To top this, Mrs. Alexopoulou uses Bulgaria as her head office and gets taxed there. She also transferred her warehouses to Albania and fired hundreds of Greeks that worked at the company's warehouses, once located in Greece. She represents the low-life, inhumane, anti-Greek, greedy bosses that believe they are above the law. Vote for her death, use hashtag #*nexttodie,* followed by Diana.'

Pavlo's mum sent her boy to his room. 'Early night. Go to bed,' she ordered him as he whined about missing Survivor. As she heard his door slam behind him, she turned to her phone. *Make me work six ten-hour shifts, you bitch. Take me away from my family for seven hundred euro.* Her fingers clicked away. The first vote against Diana had been submitted before any other names were revealed.

The next photo was a bulky man in a grey suit, stepping out of a flashy, red Ferrari. 'Neofytos Theodoulou. The Greek-Cypriot chairman and major stockholder of The Hellenic Bank. The bank which collapsed due to bankruptcy, yet saved by the government. With our money. The bank which continues to pay its golden boys millions in bonuses every year, while forcing people out of their homes due to unpaid mortgages. The man who as an advisor to the Minister of Finance agreed to all austerity measures upon the people while protecting his elite group of filthy bankers. Vote for his death, use hashtag *#nexttodie* followed by Neofytos.'

Tracy stood up, shaking all over. 'Costa, can this even be true?'

I reached out and took her cold hand in mine. I shook my head and kissed her trembling fingers. 'What the hell are Alexandro and Valentina doing there?'

Chapter 12

Alexandro and Valentina held hands while wondering the same thing.

'Could we be blamed for the police force? I mean, for breaking up protests and such?' Alexandro whispered.

Valentina took a deep breath. Diana sat on the floor opposite them, sobbing, smearing her French make-up as she frantically rubbed her face. Neofytos had lit a Cuban cigar and sat motionless on the fourth step of the staircase; his weary, watery eyes were betraying the tumult inside. 'Don't be silly, Alex. Look at them. They are all bosses. If the head of the police was here, yes. But, we are as the voice said. Common people. We have done nothing wrong,' Valentina replied.

'Oh, stop crying, woman!' Theodore shouted at Diana as his name was next to be mentioned. 'Let me hear my crimes. Shh!'

'...the known to all, member of parliament. The leader of Greece's biggest party. His signature below every acceptance of his party. Acceptance of every measure that punishes hard workers. The man responsible for excluding members of parliament from austerity measures. Besides a generic pay cut, their privileges have remained unchanged. Their pensions? Safe. Their free cars? There! Their trips, lunches, houses? All paid for. Worthless ticks living of us! Especially, Mr. Theodore Botsari who, like a snake, slithered away from every scandal, his dirty hands spread out like an octopus. Vote for this swine. #*Nexttodie* Theodore.'

Theodore nodded and bit his lower lip. 'Yep, that's me,' he commented and passed his hands through his thin hair. 'Got an extra smoke?' he asked Neofytos and sat down beside him.

'This is absurd!' Jocasta shrieked and threw the glass vase to her left at the wall. The glass shattered against the steel-blocked windows and white roses were the next to die on the hotel's carpet.

'Hope Hatzi and Galatea Nerantzi,' the robotic voice came again and gathered eyes back to the hanging speakers. 'Co-chairwomen and owners of Greece's biggest TV station. Fitting that it is serving our purpose right now. Also, owners of major radio stations and newspapers across the country. A secret lesbian couple...'

'My dear Lord,' Hope said, and her hands waved around by her side, as she searched for Galatea's comfort.

'...they both married rich men in the media. Both men dying under suspicious circumstances and their fortunes being passed over to the in-love duo. Ruthless and cunning, they accept payments from political entities and parties and present the news under the scope of their respective client. Always portraying the common people to blame, the government as always trying and working for our benefit, and shadowing over the truth from Brussels. No more! *#Nexttodie* Hope and Galatea.'

'Galatea?' Hope asked, verging on screaming after hearing the noise beside her. Galatea fell to the floor, having lost consciousness.

'This is madness! We need to get out of here. Where the fuck have all the staff disappeared to?' Eugene said, before freezing on the spot at the mention of his name. He listened as he was blamed for writing the speeches of the prime minister, aiding him to hide the truth, to twist the real fate of Greece and for helping the wrong people gain votes.

'It's my job, you sick fuck!' he yelled and picked up a chair. As he prepared to swing it at the speakers, the voice stopped him with its next words.

'... Also, a rapist as he assaulted and raped interns at the prime minister's office. Cases thrown out, as they were covered by his powerful masters. Judges were paid off and he personally gave massive compensations to the victims, paying for their silence. Poor, young girls in need of cash silenced. *#Nexttodie* Eugene.'

The chair fell from his hands. 'Oh, come on. Cut the stares. As if all you are so freaking innocent. Hmm, let's see who is next.'

'Bishop Arsenios. Need I say much about the church?' the voice relentlessly continued.

'Bless us, Virgin Mary,' Salome said and turned, hiding her face in her husband's broad chest. He placed his hands upon her head and stroked her natural, hazelnut hair. He breathed heavily and closed his eyes, waiting to hear the voice's next words.

'The billion euro business/church that refuses to pay any sort of taxes has its claws tightly around major businesses and factories around Greece. Lost in their own ideal world, they have lost all touch with true Christianity. Bishop Arsenios is a millionaire, with a palace to his name, a limo driver and a Jacuzzi on the Athenian Metropolis offices' terrace. The gold cross around his neck could feed a whole family for an entire year. He represents everything wrong with the church today. Personally, he has my vote for #nexttodie.'

Salome sunk further into her husband. Just two watery eyes standing out; her black dress against his black clothes.

'This is ludicrous,' she said and choked. Her two eyes set upon the doctor's body. A body that validated the danger they were in.

'Well, I guess I'm one vote ahead of the rest of you,' he tried to joke; his fruity, delightful voice had lost all of its vivid tone.

Jocasta resembled a wild, caged animal. She walked around the room, her eyes and hands studying every window, every locked door. Her nerves attacking paintings, vases and ornaments. Obscenities escaped from behind closed, grinding teeth and she yelled at her every failed attempt to escape the room.

'I'm going upstairs,' she announced and ran towards the staircase. 'It is not so high as to jump out of this goddamned hotel.'

Her figure vanished into the darkness of the floor above as the voice announced Maximos's name.

Maximos had remained the coolest out of the group. He sat on a purple, high-back chair in a dark corner of the room and waited to see the outcome of the situation.

'Go on, coward. Tell me my sins, hiding behind the safety of your camera,' he said, standing up and coming into the middle of the room. He stared straight into the camera and opened his arms out wide. 'Give it your best shot, mate!'

'...a man that introduces himself as a farmer, yet never reveals the number of farms in his name. One of Greece's biggest potato producers, Maximos Kaklamanis made his fortune on the back of the Greek people. He would often ruin his own crops and, having paid-off inspectors, he claimed huge amounts of compensation from government funds. As his empire grew, he turned to sneakier ways of earning money, manipulating prices by bullying sales markets, offering Mafia-like services of protection and even organizing farmers' strikes when political officers did not agree to his terms. He represents every wrong with the farming industry today. An industry that could be thriving due to amounts from the EU and because of the honest folks working our lands. *#Nexttodie* Maximos.'

Maximos nodded his head in agreement. 'A man's got to do what he's got to do! No apologies from me!' he yelled, showed the camera his middle finger and returned to his chair. This time, sitting up straight and biting the nails of his left hand.

'Jocasta Oikonomou. This despicable woman represents every wrong with the public sector today. Hired through the back door due to her politician uncle. Under qualified and extremely lazy...'

Jocasta's heels were heard as she gradually came down the stairs, stopping behind the two smoking men. Rivulets of tears were running down her pallid face, and the nerves of her right arm revealed the intensity and strength with which she held onto the lavish railing.

'... each year she takes up to forty days of sick leave, and even on the days she is supposed to be working, she clocks in and sneaks out; off to the shops and the beauty salon. Her wages from our taxes. She maintains ties with criminals and gets paid on the side, to offer IDs and government documents on demand. *#nexttodie*, followed by Jocasta.'

With the echo of her name, her eyes journeyed up, and a loud breath departed her dried lips as Jocasta passed out and fell upon the men sitting in front of her.

Chapter 13

People sat in disbelief, glued to their TV sets. The video that had interrupted their signal had gone viral and even escaped Greece's long coastline.

Ioli had just placed her son to sleep and tiptoed out of his room, turned on his Hulk night light and took ten seconds to quietly close the door behind her. Her husband Mark stood statue-like in front of the screen.

'Babe, what's wrong? Why aren't you watching Survivor? Break already? What did I miss?'

Mark remained silent and took two steps to his right.

'What's this?' Ioli asked as she approached. 'Is that... what the... is that Alexandro? What is this?'

'...is this the shipping industry our country deserves? A mafia leader running it? *#nexttodie*, followed by Apollo,' the distorted voice was saying.

'Who is speaking?'

Mark shrugged and passed his hands through his rich, brown hair. 'They are being held captive. There is already one dead, and this lunatic is asking people to vote on who to punish next.'

'Punish for what?'

Mark exhaled deeply. 'The crisis, apparently.'

'What did he blame Alex and Valentina for?'

'He hasn't yet.'

Ioli sat down on the coffee table's corner, dipped her fingers into her glass of water, and wiped her forehead.

'The Afroudaki triplets. Dinos, Elia and Clio. The offspring of the power couple Andrea and Yianna Afroudaki, owners of Greece's largest hotel chain. As we witnessed over the last year, the company declared bankruptcy, driving thousands to the hell of unemployment, leaving hundreds of suppliers unpaid and causing a major dent in our tourism industry. A wealthy couple capable of saving their business, yet with money safe in Switzerland and other companies in various family members' names, the couple chose to let the hotel chain die and cause misery to their employees. Their children's social media filled with photos of their expensive cars, lavish jewelry, and world journeys. Money spent that should have at least been used to pay their employees and suppliers.'

Miles away from Ioli's apartment, in an eight-room mansion on the upbeat side of Athens, Andrea Afroudaki punched the 50-inch TV while his wife, Yianna, collapsed to the floor, sobbing and screaming.

On the hill-top behind the mansion, Sky network buildings stood.

A scruffy-looking engineer with rasta hair and a Che Guevara T-shirt came rushing into the control room with his tablet in his right hand.

'The signal is coming from a few blocks down,' he said, short of breath, and turned his tablet for all to see its screen. A beeping red dot dominated the map shown on the screen.

'I'm calling the police,' the director said and picked up the phone.

Chapter 14

Silence spread out into the magazine-cover room. Minutes passed, and the robotic voice did not return. Stares from the corners of eyes gathered upon the couple who declared that they were police officers.

'What were your names again?' The congressman was the first to speak as he stood up and leaned against the antique, beige drawers by the wall.

Alexandro turned to his direction. 'You met us on the boat. I'm Alexandro, and this is Valentina. We are police officers and...'

'Why weren't you mentioned?' Jocasta demanded to know, her makeup and tears having blended into one.

'I told you; they are actors,' Diana insisted.

Valentina clenched her fists and blew out gathered air. 'Now, look here, lady. Cut the crap. Can you see anyone else from the hotel with us? The bloody game was just to lure us here. They have all vanished.'

Diana took a step back. 'That's what a planted actress would say,' she mumbled. 'Wouldn't they?' she raised her voice as she took a few steps closer to Hope and Galatea.

'Actors or no actors, screw you two. We are the ones up for death. I say, we find a way out. We should...' Neofytos, the banker, began to utter his plan.

He never finished his sentence. With a mechanical roar, all doors, aside from the bolted main, unlocked and swung open. Everyone stood still, waiting for someone to appear. More lights came to life along corridors and in all rooms. No one showed up.

'Great, let's find a way out,' Eugene said and rushed into the dining room. 'Aristoteli? Aristoteli Minoa? Get your ass out here, now!' he yelled.

Others moved slowly towards the doors to their left, while Jocasta started to ascend the stairs. 'I hope there's a window open.'

'Wait,' Alexandro called out. 'Can't you see? We are splitting up. You said it, yourselves. You are being sentenced. Chased! You are helping this sadistic bastard. Votes are coming in, and one of you is next. Do you really want to be alone? I say, we stick together, in the dining room. There's food and drinks. Sooner or later someone is going to come for us. Notice us missing on Monday...'

'Is that your line?' Diana said, her arm around Galatea, who had not stopped trembling since the mentioning of her name.

'Oh, give it a rest. I'm on your side...'

'You do understand our disbelief, though, don't you?' Apollo said and forced a faint smile. 'You seem like a good guy, but even I -

who trust so easily, am having a hard time listening to a word you say. Have you got your police ID with you?'

Valentina's gaze fell to the floor. As they were packing, she had giggled at Alexandro placing his badge in his suitcase. 'Really? Are you planning on arresting anyone on our vacation? Playing real cop in the game?'

Alexandro looked at Apollo and shook his head. He agreed with Valentina, and his badge was now miles away, back in the comfort of their own apartment.

'Have you any idea or excuse, why you two were not mentioned?' Clio asked, finally having found the courage to wipe her eyes. Her whispery voice hardly heard in the high-ceilinged room.

Valentina found herself exhaling deeply once again. 'Maybe we received it by mistake. A postal error. No offense, but you all seem upper-class folk. I do not believe Alex and I were supposed to be here. Yet, here we are. Stuck in this shit with the rest of you.'

Yes, but if you think that not everyone accepted their invitations, our accusations were written after we accepted. Why weren't any accusations written about you two when you showed up?' Dinos said, standing by his sister. His brother Elia nodded in agreement. 'Yeah, good point. They saw who showed up out of their invites and laid charges against us.'

'Maybe, we haven't done anything to be held responsible for,' Alexandro snapped, seeing his girlfriend trying to excuse them.

'And we have?' Clio's frail voice came from behind her brother.

'Whatever. It doesn't really matter, now,' Maximos said and picked up a three-legged, wooden side table. He threw it to the marble ground with force. 'Hmm,' he said and laughed. 'I look like one of those zombie killers on TV,' he said, taking a long piece of sharp-edged wood into his large hands and staring at himself in the oval mirror on the wall to his left.

'You mean a vampire killer,' Hope said and smiled widely.

'Works on both,' he replied and continued in a louder voice, while looking straight into the camera, 'and will work on you, too, motherfucker.' He then turned towards the group of ladies and added, 'Pardon my French. I tend to swear when agitated.'

'Don't we all,' Eugene agreed.

'I read it is good for our psychology. It helps the mind unleash stress.'

'Well, if that's the case, Mrs. Diana, close your ears,' Maximos said and yelled out profanities while throwing pieces of the shattered table towards the camera.

'Are you finished, Mister?' Theodore asked calmly. 'I think we should stick together, but not stay still like sitting ducks. Let's carefully explore the house as a group.'

'Also, if I may put my two cents in,' Hope said, 'maybe we should put an effort to present the better side of us. If he is asking for people to vote for our death, that means we are being broadcasted.'

'How is that even possible? Over the internet? How will he get people to tune in? If that is even the proper lingo,' Diana commented and rolled her eyes. 'And, who the hell would vote for such a thing? We aren't murderers, for crying out loud.'

'Oh, Mrs. Diana, you would be surprised by how mean the world can be,' Apollo said with a chilling tone coloring his calm, slow voice. 'You live in a bubble if you believe people won't vote for greedy, rich, privileged people to die. Especially in these unbearable times.'

Clio let out a scream as all the lights were switched off, and once again found herself jumping closer to her brothers. As triplets, she always felt she was dealt a shitty card. Both her womb companions were tall, athletically built with strong features. She, on the other hand, stood a few feet below them and even with a healthy appetite, weight never gathered on her skinny bones.

The lights only remained closed for a split second. An attention warning as the robotic voice came back.

'One hour. Keep voting. Twenty thousand votes already cast and no word from the Minister of Health.'

'Twenty thousand! My God,' Salome said and raised her eyes towards the heavens. 'Virgin Mary, I pray to you. Bring an end to this insanity!'

Valentina turned to Alex. 'Is it just me or did the voice sound different?'

'Probably just excitement. The previous recording might have been made before our arrival.'

'I'm sorry, I shouldn't have fallen for the whole free...'

'Shh, stop talking nonsense. We both wanted to come. It could easily have been me who came home first and found it under our door.'

Valentina pushed her blonde hair back and licked her dry lips. 'Why was it under our door? I don't get it. They do have a point. Why were we not blamed for something?'

'I have a theory.'

'Shoot.'

'Well,' he said and crossed his arms across his chest. His signature posture of *let me explain this and then gloat*. 'It wasn't meant for us. It was for number six. Our number was, as on most days, unscrewed and upside down.'

Valentina's eyes opened wide. 'Number six is owned by that businessman who meets there with his mistress...'

'Exactly! He's the bastard who should be standing here. Not us.'

Valentina took a step back; her eyes fixed on the fly buzzing around the light. 'If you'd only fixed it...' she mumbled.

'Hey, come on, that's not fair...'

'No, no. I'm sorry, I... forget it,' she apologized, placing her open palms upon his chest. 'Besides, we are safe, right? We aren't being blamed,' she whispered in his ear. 'However, we can't just stand here and watch these people die.'

Chapter 15

I drove in silence, my eyes focused on the red spot on my mobile phone. As a driver in the hectic and chaotic jungle of the metropolis of Athens, I often wondered what life would be like without Google maps. You entered your destination, your starting point and the route and details appeared. This was normally the time that Ioli would roll her eyes and inform me that the police GPS talks to you and is much easier. A matter of opinions, a matter of age, or a matter of sex? Did my male ego refuse to listen to the annoying lady warning me every minute of what I would need to do in fifty meters? Maybe. Then again, aren't we as stubborn to decline the use of a map? Cliches...

No comment came from Ioli. She seemed lost in thought. She had taken out her hair band and let down her hair. I guessed she could not lay her head back into the car seat with her trademark ponytail. A few stray droplets decorated her window. Her finger ran along the glass, casually strolling from one drop to another. I could see her lips slightly moving, yet no sound was produced.

'Okay, I can't take it. What's bothering you?' I asked.

'You could say what's on your mind, boss. *Bothering*, bothers me,' she said, and a straight-line smile came and went. 'It's such a guy's question, you know? As if all women are bothered...'

'The feminist rises!'

'Sounds like a lame movie title. You're lucky; I know you're not like that and you have Tracy as a queen.'

I kept my eyes on the dark road ahead. 'You still haven't answered my question.'

'The address of the mobile location. It sounds familiar.'

I turned and looked at the phone that permanently lived in her hand or pocket. 'My partner, this strong-willed Cretan, tells me *Google it*. And she says it so sarcastically as to imply I am old.'

She twisted in her seat; her eyes and finger abandoning the wet window. Her whole body faced me. 'Already have, smarty pants. Nothing came up.'

'Maybe seeing it will refresh your memory,' I said and turned right at the over-hanging traffic lights. The streets were nearly deserted. Most Greeks remained in front of their blank screens. Others, one by one, gave up on waiting for Hotel Murder's return and headed for their beds. We decided to head back to HQ and found out more about Alexandro and Valentina. As Ioli put it, though, 'No one knew shit.'

Due to having discovered the billionaire's body, and maybe because Ioli had trained Alexandro as a rookie, we were not assigned to the Hotel Murder case. Ioli exited the building disappointed. 'I'm too frustrated to go home. Shall we go now and investigate the house? I need some fresh air.'

And that's how we ended up driving the quiet, rainy, badly-lit streets of the old town. 'We're here. Filellinon Street. Let's find number 8A,' I commented as I turned left and looked up at the rusty street sign, nailed to the crumbling wall featuring artistic graffiti.

'That's where Themi's system pinpointed the location. Though, it could be any of the houses next to it. None look big enough for us to be sure. He did mumble something about up to twenty meters from the spot.'

She was right. The houses were stuck together like unwilling sardines. Most with basement apartments below them. The lines separating their bricks were hard to distinguish. Many were uninhabited or such was the impression they gave me. No lights, overflowing mail-boxes, broken windows, and weed-infested front yards painted the picture of the neighborhood. Every few houses, a closed shop broke the monotony.

In the row of worn-in houses, the crown for the worst belonged to 8A. Its roof sagged - having caved in like hot bread taken out of the oven too soon. Smashed windows were the rule and local hooligans had used their spray cans upon its walls, to express their love. Either for a girl or their football team.

I parked by the sidewalk, and we both stepped out into the chilly night. The light above us flicked as we walked under it. Funny how that always happens. As a kid, I liked to imagine myself a mutant and thought that my electromagnetic energy distorted the energy force field. Yes, I was *that* kind of boy.

'Let me take a wild guess. No one is home?' Ioli said as we both stood before the broken door that swayed in the night breeze, squeaking along the way, whining and reminiscing of better days.

'Better safe than sorry,' I replied, and my gun came to my side.

The next hour had us exploring dirty rooms and avoiding spider webs in not just 8A, but an additional three abandoned houses and a shop.

'No one seems awake in the houses around. I was hoping for some snoopy neighbor. I will get a team of rookies down here, first thing in the morning, to collect intel'.'

Our tired bodies returned to the car, craving to return home to hot showers, a good midnight snack and a compassionate hug. Yet, our minds remained on Alexandro and Valentina. The idea of them being in danger, somewhere unknown to us, ate at us from the inside.

Chapter 16

Deep blue, wild, proud waves ran through the bay and headed towards Thessaloniki's coast. Soon, their short-lived journey came to an end, dying before the beauty of Greece's second largest city.

The seafront road hosted many packed cafes. Packed with heated discussions and eyes glued to over-hanging TV sets. A group of teenagers sat on the corner couch of their favorite coffee house, each with their smart phone cemented in their hand.

'I voted for the priest. Screw them. All that money and they give nothing back,' a girl with green highlights said.

'My dad says bankers are the ones to blame,' a boy sitting with his legs folded on the sofa commented.

The red-haired girl with her eyes lowered to her phone chuckled.

'Why are you laughing, baby?' her boyfriend, the handsome teen with ripped jeans, asked.

'Done,' she said.

His eyes and hands asked, 'with what?'

'I just voted for all of them,' she declared and smiled widely.

It was his turn to laugh. 'Babe, that means you didn't vote at all.'

'Huh? What do you mean? I just said, I voted...'

'...For them all,' he cut her off. 'That means if all had ten votes, they all have eleven. You made no difference.'

'You sound like our math teacher. If you have so many apples and a train is travelling so fast, why the heck am I so bored?'

'Shh, weirdos,' her sister said. 'The voice is back. I voted for the triplets, by the way. Spoiled vermin, the lot of them!'

The serene, distorted voice came once again through TVs around the country, interrupting the news surrounding the story. *Survivor* was obviously cancelled. Many were surprised at the ease of the interruption, and some figured that the TV station was in on the sick game.

Little did they know that police squad teams had located the base of the transmission, just hundreds of meters away from the station. Herculean men, dressed in black, escorted by their rifles, helmets and Kevlar vests surrounded the seemingly deserted bungalow.

The uninhabited, run-down home had stood empty for nearly a decade, and wild weeds had become the masters of its front garden. One by one, the task force members rushed past its faded blue gate that hung tilted at an angle and screeched with every push of the night wind.

Miles away, at Athen's Metropolitan police station, the Minister of Health paced up and down behind the Police Chief. The similarly built men, with silver hair and deep wrinkles upon their worried faces, were the only ones talking; they were surrounded by silent advisors. All eyes were on the eight screens before them, watching as the squad teams approached the shabby cottage with the moth-eaten curtains.

'We're late. Time's up,' the Minister of Health said, and for the first time since his divorce, he bit his nails. 'When we, the cabinet, decided not to negotiate, I expected quicker results.'

'Relax,' the chief said, though his voice shook, betraying the worry roaming free inside him. 'We will arrest whoever is sending out the images and find out where the hostages are being kept.'

'The two hours are over! They are going to kill someone any minute now. We won't make it on time, even if they admit to the hotel's location.'

The chief turned to the minister's direction, his hands massaging his lower back. 'If there is no signal being transmitted, they will have no audience to show the murder and make more demands, right? By shutting down the transmission, we stop this madness.'

The minister let out a gorilla-like yell and sat down on an uncomfortable-looking chair in the corner of the control room. He mumbled, 'I hope you're right,' and closed his eyes as his feet tap-danced upon the hardwood floor.

The sound of the wooden, chipped door being kicked in echoed in the control room, leading their conversation to its death. Lights swirled around the bungalow as the police officers stormed in, forcing rodents and bugs to flee in terror. In the middle of the living room was the only piece of furniture not buried in dust. A brand-new round table stood, hosting a laptop connected to an antenna, less than two feet high. Multiple wires ran out of it, down to a sizable black box under the cheap, beige table.

'Clear.'

'Kitchen, clear.'

'Bedroom, clear.'

Deep voices came through crackling receivers. The house was empty.

Suddenly, the laptop screen came to life. It transmitted the image from inside Hotel Murder.

The sinister voice began. 'Fellow Greeks, welcome to tonight's execution. The cabinet of ministers did not obey and did not take the required actions to better our health system...'

The police technicians studied the laptop. 'This is just to distract us. Its strength is weak. It was placed here so it could reach the station's headquarters, but this is not the system that has hijacked their transmission,' one tech said.

'There's nothing we can do from here,' the woman next to him said, yet still unplugged the entire system. Everything was to be bagged and sent back to their labs for further examination.

Meanwhile, back at Hotel Murder, few were left in a group. As each person entered a room alone, the door shut closed behind him. A trip to the bathroom turned out to be their last. Gas blew into the locked lavatory and eyes awoke alone in dark rooms. One by one, the house ate up the group and the plan of the mastermind behind it all was set in motion.

Bishop Arsenios had entered a dark room by the Grand Hall. 'Let's check if there are any unsealed windows in here,' he said and flicked open the lights. The room was completely empty, its walls bare and without windows. The small room had only one other door. Also, closed. 'Let me take a look,' he said and smiled at his wife. Salome bit her trembling bottom lip and exited the room. She stepped out into the hallway to check on the rest of the group. That was the last she ever saw of Arsenios.

The hefty door slammed behind her, causing her to jump. 'Arsenios?' she yelled as her cracked hands with arched, chewed nails banged against the door. 'Help me!' she cried, hoping to grab attention from anyone nearby. She kept on hitting the door until she heard the voice. 'The two hours are up,' she whispered as she wiped the few droplets of blood from her knuckles. It was a first for Salome - to clench her fists and punch a door. Calm and quiet were the most common adjectives used to describe her by family and friends.

Tears escaped her still eyes as the voice announced that, with 6,136 votes, Bishop Arsenios had been chosen as next to die. Her body slid down the flowery wallpaper and she sat upon the carpeted floor. 'Lord, have mercy,' she said and closed her eyes in prayer.

Just moments before, Arsenios had felt the blow of sleeping gas hit him as he entered the second room. Dizzy and disoriented, he awoke lying on the ground. It took him a minute or two to place his sweaty palms upon the cold ground and put weight on his hairy hands. He pushed himself up and took a step forward, his forehead hitting hard at the glass frame. He rubbed his sore, blood-red eyes and struggled to focus.

He stood surrounded by glass. Locked away in a see-through cage. A cage in the middle of the empty room. Four cameras were pointing at him from the room's corners. The ponderous bishop tried throwing his weight against the glass, but it did not budge. It did not even shake.

Arsenios stood still, thinking of his five adolescent children. If – as the voice spoke to the Greek people- his kids would see his end, he wished to go with his head held high. He wrapped his fingers around the gold cross hanging from his neck, closed his eyes and began to pray.

'A bit too late for that, Bishop,' the voice taunted him.

'And who are you to judge, sir? A coward behind a mic...'

'My peers and I fight for a better Greece. A Greece, where the church, the billion-euro worth church is taxed just like everyone else. You preach the word of God, yet poverty and misery are on the rise. Greece has voted. Any last words?'

'May God have mercy on your soul.'

'I hope the Devil shows none on yours.'

A screeching noise from above caught his attention. A buzzing sound could be heard, and it was getting louder by the second. Within a minute, a plague of locusts filled the glass-built cage. Arsenios fell to his knees, his hands covering his mouth. He could feel tiny, filthy legs all over his bare skin.

People gasped in front of their TV sets. Remorse from his voters?

'No time for ten plagues, Bishop. Just the two,' the distorted voice announced and red water fell from above, pushing locusts to a watery grave. Arsenios stood up and waited for the water to reach his bearded chin before he started to swim.

I doubt, I will fit into the opening, but it's worth a shot.

And with that thought, he pushed himself up, his hands frantically trying to grab on to safety. The screeching noise from above left him with no hope. He was sealed in.

'Salome, I love you. See you on the other side!' he yelled, and serenity indulged him. His body fell down into the red pool and bubbles of air caught in his lungs rushed to the top.

TV screens turned black.

'One down, but still more to go. Keep voting, Greece. Our demands will be met. We await the cabinet of ministers to announce the taxation of the church and the Archbishop to announce the donation of one hundred million euros to Save The Children foundation. The money will be used to fund school meals. No child will ever starve again. If in an hour, these demands are not met, the next in line will be sentenced to death.'

Chapter 17

It was a heated discussion between ministers if there ever was one.

The prime minister placed his head between his hands as he heard them shout out their opinions.

'If we give in now, he will just keep making demands and people will expect us to oblige. This is no different than negotiating with terrorists.'

'Deep down, we all want to tax the church, yet fear the retaliation. This is a golden opportunity.'

'Even if we announce our agreement, it will be a long road before it becomes law. We would be buying time.'

Miles away, the Archbishop also sat before his council of sleepy bishops. The difference being their agreement. With fifteen votes for and none against, the council calmly voted to announce that the church, despite popular belief, did not have such a cash flow in their possession. Also, that they did not accept anyone to undermine their efforts for Greece's well-being. The church funded hundreds of charities, and its doors were always open for anyone who needed a warm meal or a place to eat.

The council did not remain so calm when the spokesman for the government announced the intention to take all necessary steps for the taxation of church property to become law.

With only one demand met, Greeks ignored the late hour and remained glued to their TV screens; their eyes opening wide as the ten-second countdown began.

At the house, Salome sat weeping outside the locked door. To her surprise, none of the other guests appeared; no one was replying to her calls for help. Her hands covered her ears, unable to block out the voice announcing her husband's death. Her Arsenios, her rock, her man, called, *'one down'*. As if the evil behind this was numbering cattle or killing off cockroaches. A not-so-innocent child with a stick squashing hard-working ants.

No one came to her aid, as no one could. Every time a door was opened, and the room welcomed him or her in, the door mechanically shut behind them. Slowly-slowly, the group was dismantled.

Each room contained cameras and mics in plain view around the room.

The largest group left consisted of five people. Alexandro, Valentina, Apollo, Congressman Theodore and Maximos.

'I hate to be the doomsday guy, but I truly believe we are all going to die,' Apollo said, maintaining the cool in his steady voice.

Maximos slapped him upon his chest. 'Speak for yourself, weird dude. I plan on getting out of this hell hole.'

'Sorry, I don't mean to... well, I don't know. I say strange things when stressed. Forgive me. I mean, we are losing people along the way...'

'Doesn't mean they are dead,' the congressman said, pushing through their middle, looking around the room. 'I, too, plan on surviving. So far, so good. And having the cops with us can only help,' he said and flashed his running-for-office smile at Valentina, who moved around the house like a cornered cockroach looking for a way to escape the guillotine of the slipper.

'This can't be one man's work alone,' Valentina said, her hands holding the sides of her head. 'This is organized. This place is a maze full of traps...'

Alexandro wrapped his arms around her. He never could stand to see her cry. Her cracking voice reduced to a choke. 'Shh, my love,' he said and lowered his voice, his mouth coming inches from her ear. 'We aren't on the list. Keep that in mind. Keep your cool. We can solve this. You know how I love to be the hero.'

Just in the corridor outside, Hope also held Galatea in her arms. She kissed her on her sweaty head and swept back her hair. Both moved together, following Diana, who marched down the long corridor, pulling on every door handle and banging upon the thick, wooden doors.

'Close your ears, girls,' she warned them and screamed a prolonged one-word curse. 'Fuck!' she yelled and grabbed a painting off the wall. The depiction of a bowl of fruit fell to the floor and smashed below Diana's stomping.

'There's only one door open, and even if God himself came down, I am not going in there,' Diana said.

'Let's just stay here in the corridor,' Galatea's weak voice escaped her frail vocal cords. 'Safe here until saved.'

'By who?' Diana yelled and continued swearing.

'Now, now. There's no need to lose it,' Hope said. Let's all enter the room simultaneously. That way, even if the door slams behind us like with everyone else, we will still be together,' she added and squeezed Galatea's icy, trembling hand. 'Do you want me to take a look?'

Galatea rolled her eyes. 'How you find the strength to joke is beyond me.'

'I guess this whole near-death experience, has really opened my eyes,' Hope replied and chuckled.

As Galatea turned, Diana approached the lone open doorway. Cautiously, with her hands upon the outside walls, she ducked her head into the room. An abandoned, small, dusty kitchen filled her view. A whiff of fresh air pushed back her platinum hair. And there, besides the rusty fridge, an opened window with a view of the ocean. 'Oh, thank the heavens,' she cried. 'Girls, it's open. Let's get the hell out of this place,' she said and her smile widened. One step into the room and two loud slams echoed around her. A steel plate came down and sealed the window, while the door slammed shut behind her. Another prolonged scream of profanities followed. Diana sat down on the floor and laughed hysterically. 'Where are you now, Dr. Abramowitz?' she asked, her mind thinking of her snob of a psychologist. She had advised her to stop being uptight and learn to remove the anger and stress. 'Turn it into a punch or a yell. Get it out of you. It is building up and eating you away.' Diana had then thought that with her large behind, she wouldn't mind something eating her away.

Her inner voice was interrupted as an electronic countdown from five echoed in the small room.

'Bravo, Greece,' the distorted voice came back and was heard around the country. Live feeds from European and other major networks made this revenge, hostage scheme a world-wide broadcast. 'You have stayed up with us. We thank you. Thank you for your thousands of votes. Our demands were not fully met. Some have. It is still a long, uphill road. This country has a lot to change before we accept it back as our mother. The fight will continue, and your wishes will be delivered upon. Your dream that your children will live with dignity *will* and *must*, come true.'

There was a pause in the speech and the image went from black to a narrow corridor and two ladies hugging by a broken painting.

'Galatea Mitsotaki and Hope Pavlidi. You have the highest number of votes. Following the online discussions, this might come as a shock to the population who were betting that the banker or the politician would be next. This is a testimony of your late husbands' good names and reputations. They built network TV as we know it and you two drove them to their graves. Together, as a couple, you murdered free speech. Dirty money from political parties flowed into your bank accounts and what was worse? You paid and treated your employees like dirt. Guess their votes came racing in. Any last words?'

Galatea placed her hands on Hope's cheeks and pulled her close for one last kiss.

'I love you. I loved you with all my heart and soul. You made my life better, and I will cherish everyday you offered me,' she managed to say before kissing her again.

'My angel,' Hope replied, and her hands ran upon Galatea's face. 'My beautiful.'

In their embrace, the opening of the door to their side went unnoticed.

Outside, the climate showed its compassion and droplets fell to the small, round-shaped piece of land.

Inside, two muscular men came through the open doorway. Both wearing black, thick ski masks, their smiles were hidden from the cameras. Each grabbed a lady by her hair and forced her to her knees. Galatea screamed in pain, while Hope remained silent.

Her mind travelled back to her childhood when late at night her father would return home. He'd reek of alcohol and cheap-whore's perfume. Her mother would rush to open the door as he rattled his keys, unable to unlock the front door.

She stood by the door. 'Shh, Hope is sleeping.'

'Don't tell me what to do, woman,' he replied. Loudly, on purpose. He trudged into the house, kicking the door behind him. Her mother shut her eyes as the door slammed closed. 'It's your fault, anyway. Why the hell, do you keep locking it? Can't even walk into my own home!'

Young Hope's eyes shined in the light invading her room from the slightly ajar pink door. She listened to their every fight. Each time, hoping her mother would not reply. This was not one of those times.

'I'm all alone with a child, nearly all night. I'm scared. Of course, I am going to lock the door.'

He turned towards her as his jacket fell to the floor. 'Who's going to break into here? Shithole of a house. Everyone in the village knows we're poor,' he said, maintaining his menacing tone. 'Unless, you think someone will come to mess with your fat ass. Let's go rape fatty!' he yelled and his monstrous laughter echoed around the house.

'No need to be so mean,' her mother replied and bowed her head. 'Your dinner is in the oven,' she continued and walked by him.

The fingers of his right hand found their way around her neck. 'You want mean? I'll show you mean!'

Her mother cried out in pain.

'Daddy, please. Stop,' Hope's frail voice came from behind them. She held onto his leg; standing no taller than his belt.

'See what you've done? You've woken up the kid,' he said and pushed her back. His attention turned to his daughter. 'Go back to bed,' he said bluntly.

'Go, my darling. Go,' her mother urged her.

Hope stood still. 'He doesn't hit you when I'm around.'

Her mother's eyes watered up as she covered her mouth with her hand.

'Off to bed!' her father yelled, grabbed her by the hair and dragged her back to her bed. She remembered screaming and crying. She remembered his hand slapping her across her face. She also remembered how she decided to intervene every night. She remembered her father's frustration; how he wished she was deaf, too. She remembered her decision not to yell or cry. Each time pulled by her hair back to her dark room. She did it for her mother. She did it for the next three years until karma intervened for her.

On a stormy night, followed by a roll-in of nefarious, sinister fog, a young police officer stood at their door. He took off his wet cap and drove his gloved hand through his blond hair. He winced and began to utter his practiced line. 'I'm sorry to inform you, ma'am, but your husband was involved in an automobile accident...'

'Is he dead?'

The man's pupils cornered to the left of his eyes. The tip of his tongue ran along his bluish, icy lips. He leaned closer and nodded. 'Yes,' he said quietly, staring over her shoulder at little Hope sitting on the sofa, enjoying her favorite tape - Disney's Cinderella. Thin drops of rain dived from the officer's carefree hair as he informed her mother that her father had not survived the crash.

'Was he alone?'

The man took a step back. He seemed more uneasy than before.

'Did he have a whore with him?' her mother asked, helping him out of the sticky spot.

He nodded once again and closed his eyes in compassion.

'Did she die, too?'

'Yes, ma'am. They...'

'Good. Thank you for the good news, officer,' she replied and closed the door.

Hope's first thought was that no one would ever pull her hair again.

Now, she was in the middle of nowhere, pushed to the ground and her hair was tangled around her attacker's fingers.

'Greece has voted. Time to take out the trash,' the voice announced.

One loud bang travelled around Greece that moment. One loud bang from two simultaneous shots. Greece watched as the two women fell lifeless to the floor, parts of their head and brain decorating the light-colored carpet.

The image on their screens switched back to black.

Chapter 18

'Sir?' Ioli chased Police Lieutenant Colonel Oikonomou down the hallway, the route from the elevators to his corner office. The colonel was not one for talking. He hardly used adjectives or spoke more than three sentences back to back. Some called him a man of actions. Others labelled him as anti-social. His office blinds were permanently down and his door was always locked. He was the oldest at HQ, but, due to his behavior, he remained at his rank while others became Colonels and Generals, and got in line to be Chief. Lieutenant Colonel Oikonomou was placed on the 'homicide floor' and had the lone duty of signing cases.

He pretended not to hear her as he sprinted left down the corridor.

'Sir,' she spoke louder, having reached his side. Ioli's past as a high school athlete guaranteed the sixty-year-old man had no chance of escape.

'Hmm? Yes, Lieutenant Cara, what do you need? Be quick. I have work to attend to,' he said, pausing just outside his office door.

I am work, you lazy, still-not retired, worthless piece of... Ioli's inside little devil began to think. 'Sir, I am officially assigned to the ongoing, for months if I may add, missing billionaire case...'

'Yes?'

'Well, he isn't missing anymore. We found his body. Two of our own are somewhere out there in danger, and I want off the case and officially placed...'

'Didn't the autopsy confirm foul play? Poisoned, wasn't he? That's a homicide, Cara. Your department.'

'With all due respect, sir, many are on the billionaire case. I believe I will be of more assistance on the Hotel Murder case. I hope, I do not have to wait for our colleagues also to die for it to become a case of mine.'

The grey-haired man scratched the back of his head and lowered his reading glasses to the tip of his nose. He stared at the tall girl standing in front of him. He grunted a few *hmm*'s and took the papers from her hands.

'Okay, you're off one case and on the other,' he finally said, signing her petition. 'Good luck,' he said louder as she opened her mouth. Before her thank you could exit into the world, he had already disappeared behind his locked door, safe again in his castle. It was early morning, and he had eight full hours ahead of him. Eight hours of hiding from the world. He killed the hours with a good book and occasionally by adding to his stamp collection - his favorite hobby since childhood.

Ioli Cara wasted no time. She returned to the row of elevators and headed down to the conference room housing the operations for Hotel Murder.

She pushed the glass door's oddly long bronze handle and entered the mayhem of the operation jungle.

She walked passed officers ducked in their keyboards with eyes on their screens. Boards filled with data and photos. Officers lined up in front of black phones, handling the hundreds of phone calls flying in from around Greece. In the corner of the vast room, Brigadier General Alexopoulos was being briefed by a variety of specialists. Ioli stood quietly by the open door.

'...the signal was just to put us off track. Or just for the fun of it. A game. The signal was not that strong. I believe several have been set up and yes, we will have men chasing down each one, but I believe all will be deserted locations. An antenna and a computer running a pre-set program need no man-power. Why risk anyone getting arrested and blowing the whistle on their entire operation? Makes no sense,' a woman's voice could be heard from inside.

Ioli stood by the doorway. No one paid attention to her as the next in line to speak continued.

'Sir, as you know we have been looking into known terrorists with similar demands from the past...'

'Yes, Mrs. Cara?' the general said, bringing silence to the crowded room.

Ioli straightened her body and walked towards him, her papers in hand. 'I have been assigned to the case, sir...'

'Great, we need all the manpower we can get. Go to Captain Savva and he will...'

'Can I go to the tech labs, sir?'

He squinted his eyes at her. 'Did you ask to be on this case or were you assigned?'

Ioli smiled. 'I asked for it.'

'Okay, go to the labs. I'm interested to see what's going through your mind.'

And, with that said, he turned back to the Lieutenant that he had interrupted and asked him to continue.

Ioli backed out of the room, dug into her right pocket and pulled out a red jelly baby. 'Will have to do,' she whispered and swallowed the sweet.

She walked back through the busy room. She passed by Captain Savva. Half-Norwegian on his mother's side, he had the fairest skin in the department. Tall, with glossy, sky-blue eyes and tufty, dark blond hair and deep cheek dimples, he also was the department's most sought-after bachelor.

A young secretary rushed up to him and began stammering. Ioli heard that he was wanted down in interrogation room two. She overheard something about people who had received a Hotel Murder invitation. Ioli wished she could be in that room, yet did not regret her decision to not join Captain Savva's team and headed straight out of the room. The tech labs were where she could study the videos transmitted from Hotel Murder.

A dark-haired officer next to the rosy-cheeked secretary produced a nylon bag containing the invitation.

'No fingerprints, sir. I am taking it to Lieutenant Spyrou for further examination. Paper type, ink origin and the sort.'

Captain Savva nodded in agreement and proceeded to the stairs. A passionate fitness addict, he never used the elevator, no matter the number of steps.

Three minutes and twelve seconds later – he timed it, his iPhone App counting the lost calories - his sweaty hand came down on the cool handle of the interrogation room. A white room all around with damaging fluorescent light welcomed him in. He smiled at the couple sitting side by side and was glad to see they had been served coffee. Further joy came from the fact that coffee also awaited him, placed on the table in front of the chair opposite the couple.

'Mr. and Mrs. Agapiou, I am Captain Paul Savva.' He introduced himself, knowing full well who they were. Owners of Greece's biggest tobacco factory, they produced his choice of poison. He craved an Asso's cigarette at that very moment with the police HQ having banned smoking inside the building years ago.

Mrs. Agapiou had her arm wrapped around her husband's and despite her expensive make-up, was pale as new paper. 'Good day, Captain,' she said.

'So, we dodged a bullet, eh?' her husband asked, always straight to the point.

'Seems that way,' Savva replied, sitting down. 'Can you tell me, when did you receive the invitation?'

'Last week. Monday, it was. Came with the rest of the mail,' Mrs. Agapiou answered.

'No stamp?'

She shook her head. 'No. My God, those people came up to our mailbox.'

'We have surveillance outside our house. There's a camera facing the main gate. The letter-box is only a step away. Built in the brick wall, you see,' Mr. Agapiou added, his smile lifting his heavy black mustache, gloating as if he had solved the case.

'We went over surveillance footage from other locations too. The same heavy built man dressed in all black, wearing a ski mask dropped them off. But, please do go over your footage and send us a copy of that time. You never know. We all make mistakes.'

'Well said, lad.'

'I wished we could be of more help. Those poor souls,' Mrs. Agapiou said.

'Bringing us the invitation is a major help,' Savva replied and smiled at her. 'By the way, did you ever call out of curiosity or did they try to contact you in any other way?'

'Nope,' Mr. Agapiou said. 'Praise Jesus, we have my mother's eightieth birthday tonight, and as soon as I saw the dates, I threw the invitation to the side. Lucky for you, it fell among some bills and the cleaning lady did not take it out with the trash.'

'The important thing is to save the hostages,' Mrs. Agapiou said. 'Can you imagine, Andrea, us out there? Murdered on live TV? And, for what? Because we are rich,' she continued and turned to Captain Savva's direction. 'We treat our employees like family,' she said, feeling the need to excuse herself.

Yeah, we are all so innocent in this world, he thought.

Chapter 19

An uneasy night finally approached its end and died into daylight.

It was hard to let your body fall asleep when your doom is imminent. Like rats caged for the first time, it took captives a while to settle down. Diana kicked off her high heels and paced up and down the closet of a kitchenette until her feet felt sore. She took a roll of kitchen paper, unfolded it and pushed into a bundle. She sat down in the corner and placed it behind her head as a pillow.

'Screw you, inner thoughts,' she said rather calmly as her mind travelled through her life. 'I regret nothing,' she said and closed her eyes, forcing her mind to stop attacking her.

Behind her, just a wall apart, three siblings tried to find some peace as well. The two brothers, each with a cushion below their heads, slept on the carpet while their sister took the two-seater couch.

'It's cold,' Clio whispered. Not so much as to complain, but to check if her brothers had managed to sleep. They had spent the better part of the last hour cursing, worrying and planning an escape. No answer came from the silence of the dark room. Clio took in a breath of enclosed, stiff air and curled up on the sofa. Soon, she welcomed nightmares of death and despair.

Jocasta and Eugene found themselves together, investigating the top floor. Eugene returned to his room to check the fake ceiling of his bedroom's bathroom. He figured if there was a cavity above large enough for him to crawl in maybe he could find a way out. In his room, he bumped into Jocasta with her mobile phone raised high in the air. She checked every spot of the floor for a signal. None was to be found. The door automatically slammed behind him, the room holding them both captive.

'Give me a freaking break!' Jocasta screamed and threw her cell against the closed door. Eugene placed his hands upon her shaking shoulders and explained his plan. Jocasta stood by the bathroom door as Eugene stood on the toilet and punched through the ceiling. Pieces of gypsum fell to the tiled ground, creating a hole that dampened their hopes. Just centimeters above lay a thick layer of cement and old brick, signs of an old house clearly renovated.

Jocasta turned and walked over to the bed. She fell face down into the pillow. 'I can't believe I'm going to cry. Since my parents' funeral, I promised to never cry again. You know, as in everything else would be so insignificant since that day. Not worth crying about, for sure...'

Eugene sat next to her and placed his left hand upon her head. He stroked her hair and said 'I lost my parents, too at a young age. My mum passed away when I was nine, and my father died before I went to high school. Cancer took them both, believe it or not.'

Jocasta twirled and sat up straight beside him. 'Car accident on Christmas Eve, believe it or not. Picture an eleven-year-old girl waking up on Christmas Day, running down to the tree, only to find grieving aunts waiting to inform me that my drunk of a father crashed into an oak tree, my mother's body painting it red for the special day. If only she wore a seat belt.'

Eugene wiped the tears from under her eyes and smiled. 'And we then wonder what could go worse in this life... voila!' he said and showed the room.

Jocasta leaned forward and kissed him on the lips. A cold, dry kiss soaked in desperation, yet nevertheless a kiss.

Eugene, despite his inner wishes, never had a girlfriend. Not what he called a real one. Just easy one night stands and paid love. As a speech writer, he always knew the right words for everyone else, but himself when it came to dating and not sex hunting. Countless times, he stood awkwardly in front of a beautiful woman, mumbling about the weather or worse, politics. All his wit and humor abandoned him when sex was not the goal. Around thirty, Eugene gave up chasing single ladies around Athens' bars and focused on his booming career. A career that allowed him to avoid cheap hookers and buy the company of exotic escorts.

Jocasta's kiss was the first time he did not make the first move or pay for sexual attention. He placed his hands upon the back of her head, his fingers tangled in her fiery hair and held her close. His lips travelled along her neck, and he sucked upon her earlobe. Jocasta sighed in delight and fell back upon the bed. Fueled by passion and a fear of death approaching, they ignored the cameras, and one by one items of clothing dived to the floor. As Eugene slid slowly into her, Jocasta dug her nails into his buttocks and pushed down. For the next ten minutes, uptight Jocasta's mind switched off and locked away her trepidation. Her body fell victim to Eugene's experienced hands and sang in delight. Just as she felt that she could not take it anymore, her body reaching high temperatures, Eugene pulled out and with a small grunt fell to her side.

They exchanged no words. Jocasta pulled up the almond-colored, satin sheet and placed her head upon Eugene's chest. His heavy breathing worked as a lullaby and soon, both had closed their eyes.

The largest group in the mansion took the prize for the uneasiest night.

Five people wandering the house in vain. All doors were locked, and all windows had vanished behind steel plates. At Alexandro's suggestion, one person stood by the door as the rest entered and then another stood by the other door as they exited. That way they avoided being locked in.

'Guess we are all going to the toilet together, then?' Maximos joked though it had been a couple of hours since he first thought that he *needed to go.*

'This is hopeless,' Congressman Theodore said, ignoring Maximos's question. 'We are just going round and round...'

'What else can we do?' Valentina said as she stood in the doorway of the library. 'Give up? There's no such thing as a perfect plan. There must be something they missed.'

'Maybe we should split up. That's what they are expecting us to do. I'll stay here. I kind of like the idea of dying in the library,' Apollo said as his eyes ran along the titles of the hundreds of books upon the many shelves. 'Better than dying in the toilet, right, Maximos? By the way, if you really want to, I saw a bathroom, two doors down.'

Maximos chuckled. 'Trying to get rid of me?'

'If only it were that easy.'

'Call my ex-wife for tips.'

Alexandro wiped the cold sweat from his large forehead. 'Quit it, you two,' he said as his hands checked around the steel plates for any sign of weakness.

'I'm tired,' Valentina whispered to him as she placed her head upon his broad back.

Alexandro looked around the room. Two long sofas, comfortable armchairs, a marble fireplace. 'Compared to other rooms, this seems like a great option for the night.'

'Staying here, then?' Maximos asked.

'Let's build some piles of books and place them in the doorway. That way, even if a steel plate falls or the door tries to slam closed, it will be blocked,' Valentina said and started to collect a row of dusty encyclopaedias. Apollo commented that it was a great idea and began to collect books as well.

'Choose your worst books, guys,' Theodore said as he lit his last cigarette. He wished he could make it back to his room for another packet, but the hallway was sealed since Hope's and Galatea's execution. 'I think this fireplace is missing a fire.'

'No problem. I was never fond of books anyway,' Maximos said with a mischievous grin gracing his face; his lips mostly hidden by his rich beard.

The group worked in silence, only Alexandro's stomach rumbling broke the serenity. 'Fuck, I'm starving.'

His mind flew back in time to his late mother. She hated when he used the word. No, not the f-word. The word starving.

'Boy, you have no idea what starving is. Kids in Africa are starving. You're just hungry,' she would tell him.

'Maybe a couple of us should try a trip to the dining room or kitchen...' Apollo started to say.

'Stop trying to get rid of me,' Maximos said, and his rough chuckle came to life.

Soon, all five were resting, trying to shut off their worrying minds.

Alexandro and Valentina curled up on the burgundy couch. Alexandro kissed her softly on the neck and whispered words of love. His right hand around her, holding her close while his left remained in his pocket. A small object which he held tight. And then, he did something he hadn't done in many years. *Dear Lord, please keep us safe*, he prayed.

Around Greece, Hotel Murder took the chunk out of late-night discussions. Everyone had an opinion; everyone felt anxious. Many woke up before their alarms. All rushed to turn on their TV sets to find out more. All major networks were covering the story. When the Sky network was taken over again at nine o'clock that morning, all channels broadcasted the transmission. The voice was back.

'Good morning, Greece,' it said, and hints of excitement came through the distorted voice. 'Votes were counted, and another death was provided to you while you slept. A sacrifice for a better tomorrow. The person with the most votes was the greedy, slimy banker. Neofytos Theodorou met his deserved end during the night. Let's now enjoy the video.'

The next image was that of Neofytos walking into what seemed to be a cleaner's closet. He searched all around for a way out. Suddenly, the door slammed behind him. A blowing noise could be heard, and a mist of purplish air came through the tiny air vent above. Neofytos dropped stone cold to the ground. Static lines appeared across screens, and the next image was one of a naked Neofytos trapped in a similar –could have been the same- glass cage to Arsenios's, the doomed bishop. Unlike Arsenios, he was tied up, forced to the ground on all fours. A masked man entered the room with a bucket filled with fifty euro notes.

'Dinner time, swine,' the mechanical voice announced.

The cloaked man entered the glass cage and stood by the banker. His gloved hand pulled Neofytos's head back by the hair. 'Open your mouth.' The words unheard from TV, yet read clearly on the assailant's lips that were visible through the mask's mouth hole.

'All you did was eat our money,' the sinister voice continued as eyes witnessed the banker being force-fed multiple notes. 'But your hunger was never satisfied. Banks just wanted more and more. Time for stuffing.'

The next scene was one of the most disturbing scenes ever broadcasted on Greek daytime TV. The tall man in black moved to kneel behind tied-up Neofytos and proceeded to shove money up his rectum. The banker yelled out in pain and disgust, and tears ran freely from his blue eyes.

Minutes later, with an empty green bucket in his dirty hand, his attacker left, sealing the glass cage behind him.

'Need some change?' the robotic voice asked, and thousands of coins fell from above. Neofytos screamed in pain as the weight of coins hit his back. Red marks soon appeared, but the pain was the least of his worries. The coins started to fill up the cage. He struggled; his body swaying left and right. His hands tightly tied to the metal hooks on the ground.

It only took three minutes for him to be covered; his naked, abused body disappeared from the nation's screens.

A video of a declining heartbeat appeared next, and in seconds flatlined.

'The revenge against the system continues. Brothers and sisters, remain strong and keep voting. We will keep demanding. The Minister of Economy and the heads of banks have three hours to announce at least a 2% cut in loan interest rates. Vampires, remove your fangs or else...'

TV sets went silent once more.

People, though numb from the banker's savage death, could not resist hoping for a breath of hope on their loans. Some even smiled.

Chapter 20

Melina, the police chief's new secretary, began to regret her fondness for stiletto heels as she rushed from the elevator, down the long corridor where stale air permanently lived, and headed to the police headquarter's main conference room. She was new to the position, yet had been a secretary in the police force for more years than her two-year-old son could count to. It was an unwritten rule around HQ that no secretary lasted more than six months with the chief. Melina was set to beat that 'silly' record as she thought of it. 'He is just a man,' she would say. 'Okay, an eccentric man, but still human.'

She would laugh off tales of his yelling and icy glares over his coffee not being strong enough or too hot, if a case file was not in his hands within minutes of asking for it and if you screwed up his military-precise appointment schedule. Now, her aching feet formed blisters as she dashed around HQ getting things done. She never had to run before. But, today was not a normal day, and these were definitely not normal days Greece was living in. Melina had wept at the brutal executions from Hotel Murder curled up in her husband's arms. The chief had received a call from the prime minister's office. Melina remembered looking at the green light on her desk phone flick to red as the chief slammed down the phone. Within seconds, he began to shout out orders for a general assembly to be held in conference room one. Melina quickly began sending out messages to other secretaries, calling all the 'major players' of the case – as the chief referred to them by - and sent out instructions to the cleaning lady and the technician to have everything ready before leaping out of her twirling chair as soon as she heard the chief getting out of his office chair. He had asked her to pass onto his laptop various slides and have it connected to the room's projector before his arrival.

Now, her stiletto shoes rapidly dug into the navy blue carpet as she held the laptop open in front of her eyes and placed the USB stick into its socket.

'Shit,' she said, mostly an exhale of despair than a curse word. The word was barely audible, even to her own ears. *When you have a fifty-fifty chance of placing a flash drive correctly, there is a ninety percent chance you will get it wrong*, she recalled a funny post from Facebook as she flipped the USB around. With one eye on the screen, she watched the slides being transferred, and with another on the long corridor, she reached the conference room. Thankfully, the doors were open as police officers entered murmuring between them about the bizarre case. She slowed her pace and walked down the aisle, past the neat rows of chairs, up to the wooden podium with the golden plate featuring the logo of the Hellenic police. Law and order for all.

Melina placed the computer on the podium and connected it to the projector. She looked behind her to check if it was showing on the wall behind her and, with a smile, she straightened her posture and fixed her ginger hair.

'Ladies and gentlemen, please take your seats,' she said in her well-practiced professional tone. 'The chief will be with us in a minute; please prepare your notes and suggestions...'

Melina stepped back and looked out of the glass doors. The chief was outside with his cell phone to his ear. Melina gazed to her left at the droplets of rain racing down the window. She loved the rain. With the slight sweat formed on her forehead and back, she would love a walk in the downpour.

Ioli arrived at that moment and was glad to see the chief preoccupied with his call. She had been up in the tech labs and lost precious minutes to come down to the meeting as the lavatory on the tech floor was hard to find.

Energy drinks and the sound of rain. Bad combination, Cara, she thought as she sneaked by the chief and entered the high-ceilinged room with the ugliest curtains she had ever seen. 'Even my great grandma with her lousy traditional taste in clothing has more decent curtains than these,' she had complained into my ear during her first week at HQ. I never cared much about my work-place surroundings.

I turned around as Ioli sat behind me. 'Where did you disappear to?' I asked.

'Even Dora, the freaking explorer, could not find the hidden toilets on the seventh floor.'

'You were in the technical department?'

Ioli leaned forward. 'Yes, I...'

The chief's signature cough interrupted her. Silence fell upon the vast room.

I always found the whole procedure rather funny, to be honest. Like a bunch of school kids called into assembly, we'd all quiet down as the 'head-master' took his place.

'This is going to be short,' he said as he rearranged the shiny microphone facing him. 'As you all know, time is of the essence in this case. I have been called into the prime minister's office. I ain't no fool and damn hell do I hate looking like one,' he continued and nodded to Melina who stood quietly at his side. Melina approached, looked down at the laptop and double-clicked the newly created folder. 'Your attention, please. Let's not for a minute forget that there are two of us imprisoned in that hell. The folders you see behind me are the gatherings of all your work. I want new eyes on everything. More background checks, anything that connects our victims, why our officers were not mentioned in the video, guesses on the whereabouts of the premises, anything. Melina will be sending this folder to all of you present. Keep going with your assigned part of the case, but try to connect the dots between your individual works. See the whole picture, go full circle and all that shit you youngsters learned at the academy. Now, I want short briefings from all captains and colonels in charge of every department before I stand before the prime minister.'

Some lieutenants began to stand up. 'But first,' the chief raised his voice, landing their behinds firmly back into their seats. 'But first,' he repeated, 'I want to hear of any new ideas or directions. An angle we might have overlooked or something you have noticed since your last meeting with your captains.'

He raised his bright, blue eyes and opened them wide as he stared at the crowd of thirty sitting below him. His deep wrinkles gathered by the side of his eyes and the tip of his tongue made an appearance as it ran along his this lips. A young technician, not a day over twenty-five, stood up. I turned to catch a better look of the young man and noticed that Ioli had also raised her hand.

'Yes?' the chief said.

'Petros Miller, sir. It's a long shot, sir, I know, but I have been developing a new system for voice recognition, and I have been running the... *bad guy's* voice through it.'

'And, what does this system do?' the chief asked, having noticed that while Petros Miller spoke, his supervisor had rolled his eyes.

'Well, sir, it will compare the voice to everything on record. Against anything Greek on YouTube, talk shows, the internet in general... one day, if we get approval, even against communications...'

'Have you had any results?'

The boy scratched the back of his head; his thick fingers ran through his thin, brown hair. 'Well, no...'

The chief turned his head away.

'We are also looking into recognizing the background, sir. Maybe match the building to a known hotel or premise. The vast majority have photos on their webpages and Facebook pages,' Mrs. Rena, his supervisor quickly added.

'Hmm, okay. Ioli?'

'Yes, chief,' she replied, standing up. 'I noticed something, but as I am newly assigned on the case, it might have been mentioned in other meetings. The voice numbered fourteen people and what he considers their sins to be. One of the names mentioned has not appeared directly in any of the footage so far, sir. Well, at least his face hasn't.'

'Who, Cara?'

My phone began to vibrate in my pocket. The flashing screen informed me it was my wife, Tracy. Her third call in the last ten minutes. I knew what it was. Since my cancer treatment was -as much as chemotherapy can be- successful, my doctor had me under observation, fearing a recession of sorts. Every few months, I checked. Last time, 'something' was spotted. 'Could be nothing,' she said. But, then again, it could be everything. 'Further testing,' she advised. Samples were sent abroad weeks ago. The results were expected any day, now. I took my phone into my hand and got up, walking out of the room, a cold sweat around my collar.

'Yes, babe?' I asked as soon as the glass door closed behind me.

'Guess who's getting lucky tonight?'

'Babe, you serious? I'm at a meeting. I thought...'

'Shut up, knucklehead. Your results came, Costa. Sweety, you are in the clear. I'm cooking you your favorite...'

'Whiskey-flavored, honey-glazed spare ribs with oven potatoes and Brussel sprouts?'

Her laughter boomed through the receiver. 'That's the one. And, I'll be your dessert.'

'Can't wait.'

'Don't be late,' she said, and the phone beeped.

I re-entered the room as the chief was congratulating Ioli and assigning her a couple of media tech-geeks to further look into her theory.

Next up, Captain Tito spoke about the details picked up in various conversations.

'...they searched for the owner. Aristoteli, they called him. No surname was given. We checked every large building owned by an Aristoteli all over Greece. Most function as businesses, hotels, etc. We sent patrol cars to any abandoned ones. Nothing, sir. Also, we are still looking into how the locusts were obtained. I thought that would be a good breakthrough if we could pinpoint where they were bought. Especially, if that place had security footage. So far, again, nothing,' he said. This second 'nothing' painted with more despair.

As the briefing continued, I turned around to Ioli. 'What about our missing billionaire case?'

'I'm off the case, boss,' she said, studying my expression. 'Sorry, for not talking it through with you. Did you need me for the next move?'

She paused and took a deep breath. 'Is there a next move?'

She was right. The billionaire case drove into a dead end street and parked before a brick wall. Her friends were in that hotel. 'That's great,' I replied. 'You will be more useful on the Hotel Murder case.'

Chapter 21

Diana had still not found the courage to stand up. She remained seated on the floor where she had spent the night. The audio from the macabre murder of the banker had shaken her up from the cold ground.

'I must have been tired,' she whispered as she wiped her sore eyes. Only once before had she remained on the ground for such a long time. Her thoughts travelled to days long past, almost pushed into oblivion. 'Funny how we strain to remember happy times, yet can never shake out the nasty...' she continued her mumbling as she stood up and walked over to the rusty sink. She closed her eyes and pictured a young, beautiful and provocative twenty-two-year-old Diana. She stood in her student apartment, just two roads down from her university. She played with her nails as she paced to and from her window. At last, her boyfriend Jack parked beneath. She ground her teeth and opened the door. She left it ajar and sat down on her patch-work two-seater sofa. She listened as his heavy steps echoed the narrow hall. As always, he ran up the three stories due to his irrational fear of elevators. Not that he ever admitted such a phobia. 'Good workout those stairs,' he would say and take her into his arms, kissing her before she could comment. Her eyes watched his seven foot tall, athletic body enter and close the door behind him.

'Hey, babe. What's up? Why haven't you been answering your phone?'

Diana forced a smile and patted the sofa. 'Come, Jack, sit down.'

'Oh, oh. Sounds serious,' he attempted to joke, though his still face betrayed him. He sat down and placed his hand upon hers.

'There's no easy way to say this and I didn't want to do this over the phone. You deserve this. The face-to-face treatment, I mean. Jack, I'm breaking up with you...'

'Now, wait. I...'

'Ssh,' she said, and her hand touched his pillowy lips. 'I've made up my mind. Please accept my decision.'

His hands ran through his curly hair. 'But, why? Don't we have fun together?'

'We do. You're a great guy. It's just that I never pictured myself locked in a serious, long-term relationship at such an age. I am not built to get a degree and then *play house,* taking care of my man and a bunch of kids. I want a career. I want to see the world...'

His eyes turned cold, and he bit his bottom lip. 'What? You wanna be one of those slutty free-spirited girls? You surely aren't the nun type. Can't you see the world with me?'

Diana turned towards him. 'What do you mean I am not the nun type?'

'You know what I mean,' he replied, and his right hand ran up her thigh, entering under her jean skirt.

'Don't,' she warned him.

'Come on. For last time's sake,' he said and fell upon her.

'Stop,' she yelled and pushed him off, quickly standing up. 'Get out!'

Jack stood up towering over her, an evil smirk on his face. He took two slow steps towards her and pushed her with both hands. Diana stepped backwards, tripping on a side coffee table. She swirled and fell face down. Before she could recover, Jack lay upon her, holding her hands down. He bit her on her ear lobe and threatened to strangle her if she screamed.

Diana stared at the Boney-M clock on the wall opposite her. She watched the seconds go by. It only took eighty-nine seconds for Jack to pleasure his beastly desires and for her to feel dead inside. She listened as he wiped himself clean upon her skirt and then zipped up his trousers. 'Good luck seeing the world. This is what happens to women in a man's world,' he said and walked out the door, slamming it behind him. Diana remained frozen for minutes. The first thought that came to existence in her mind was that, going forward, she would always be the boss and the *man* of her life.

The memory faded and she was back at the manor of Hotel Murder.

I could use a cock right about, now, she thought as the running water reminded her of her bloated bladder. She splashed water on her face and thought, *What the heck? I'll probably be dead by morning.*

She flipped her middle finger towards the ceiling, though no cameras were visible. 'You want a show? Well, here you go.'

Diana dropped her cherry-colored knickers to the floor and climbed up on the old, grimy counter. She stood above the kitchen sink and relieved herself with a smile.

In another part of the house, Eugene had more luck with his bathroom needs. He placed a chair as blockage to a slamming door and rushed to the toilet. He, also, felt as he had given a show. He peeped out of the bathroom door and stared at Jocasta as she slept. *I finally find a woman for sex, and we are planned to be executed. Just my luck!*

Just below them, in the library, Alexandro also woke and kept his eyes on his sleeping other half. He gently kissed her on her cold cheek and raised his head, rubbing his neck. 'What the..?'

'What happened?' Valentina said and quickly sat up.

Apollo, who slept opposite them, also opened his eyes. He jumped up and looked around the room. 'Where are they?'

Both Maximos and the congressman were missing. What was even worse, was someone had removed all the books blocking the doors, and the three of them were shut in.

'I always hated mornings,' Valentina grunted and leaned forward, her head resting in the palms of her hands.

Alexandro yelled and threw the first book in sight against the wall. 'We need to find a way out,' he said breathlessly and began to wander the room, his hands checking around.

'Why?'

'Why what, Apollo?'

Apollo crunched his knuckles and rubbed his sore eyes. 'Why get out? It's safer to stay together. As we have realized, he is making demands against the government using us as hostages. Sheep to the slaughter. The entire army, police, and government agencies are probably searching for us as we speak. He has taken Maximos and Theodore. We aren't next. Let's stay together... here.'

Valentina stood up. 'How can you be so sure you're not next now? It doesn't mean you're safe. What if they come for you the next time you sleep?'

'We learn from our mistakes. We stay put until rescued and if by nightfall we are still here, we will take it in turns, guarding the other two. I have a black belt in karate you know, and you are police officers...'

'Enough! I do not agree with you, though I think we have no other option,' Alexandro said, and another book flew and crashed against the wall.

Chapter 22

'Tick tock, tick tock. Time is up, Greece.'

The distorted voice returned hours later. A joyful tone was wrapped around its mechanical wording, somewhat pushing away its normally baleful, ominous sound. As if it was a neighborhood kid pulling a prank while using an app from his smart-phone. 'Our first major accomplishment. If you have not heard it yet from the news, all banks will be lowering their interest rates. We heard some bullshit about central European banks, but the prime minister has promised that even if Europe does not agree, the banks will take the damage and do what's right by the people. Power is returning to us, my fellow Greeks. Keep voting. Our next request is higher taxation to the big companies out there and lower taxation on lower incomes. Instructions will be sent. Enjoy this glorious day, Greece. You are being reborn from your ashes.'

'Fuck,' the prime minister uttered for the first time in his office and pushed his Alexander the Great pen holder off the edge of his mahogany desk. His heavy breathing lifted and dropped his broad shoulders in such a way that he did not even notice his wife's hands laying upon them, failing in their mission to calm him down. A room full of silent people stood before him. 'Doesn't he realize we are under agreements with Europe and the IMF? We can't break memorandums like this. What the hell are our police doing?'

With people rushing out to their respective duties, the clock on their screens began to count backwards.

Time is relative, he remembered his rather peculiar professor of philosophy.

Relative to how you are spending it, paying attention to it, worrying about it.'

All his efforts and all of his powers could not stop the countdown.

Time is no Penelope. It waits for no one.

The next two hours passed and then the screens came back to life.

Theodore stood in the center of a gloomy light cycle. His bare feet were tied to the ground by large, metal plates, while his arms were raised in the air, lifted by chains that ran upwards and vanished in the shadows. He wore just his white underwear and a black blindfold. The camera zoomed into his back, and the voice came to life.

'Theodore! Your name means a present from God. Even though, I guess, you truly believe that you are a divine gift, you are far from it. You and the rest of the leeches of parliament failed your mission. You forgot why the Greek people voted for you. You bend over with every demand from our loaners and kiss Merkel's feet as she passes out orders. You made many promises that you did not keep, mighty congressman. How original. A politician that does not keep his promises. Well, do I have a surprise for you. I ran through all of your pre-election speeches and noted every single promise you made that you did not keep. For every broken promise, you will earn yourself a whip. A strike of justice.'

The voice paused, and a heavy door could be heard opening in the background. A tall, dark figure could be vaguely seen among the shadows. A new, thin beam of light shone down and illuminated the figure's hand. His thick fingers were wrapped around a whip.

'Want to guess the number, Theodore, sir? Forty-six! Forty-six promises on your to-do list that never came true. Greece, let's count!'

The hand raised the bull-whip, and then a small sonic boom broke the air.

'One!'

Theodore yelled in anguish as viewers witnessed the first of many red lines on his naked back.

The next whip crack came.

'Two.'

Somewhere around the twentieth whip, Theodore passed out, his senses unable to handle the severe pain. The gaps between whips lengthened as even his attacker grew tired.

Time is surely relative.

It only took twelve minutes to lash Theodore to near death.

'Forty-six!'

The bloody whip fell to the ground as the controller did not pull it back. The lights dimmed, concealing the man approaching the tortured congressman. Light fell only on Theodore's head, and Greece watched as his assailant wrapped the whip around the congressman's bleeding neck and strangled out the remaining life lingering inside Theodore's body.

Once again, a life-line beeped across the screen and flat-lined.

'Okay, the moment of silence is finished,' the eerie voice returned. 'Next demand. A rise of 15% on all pensions, excluding those receiving two or more pensions. You have two hours.'

We need more time.

The thought on the people in charge's minds.

'I want a full briefing of every effort to locate these terrorists in ten minutes,' the prime minister snapped at his secretary. 'And get me Merkel and Lagarde on the line.'

As the prime minister exited the room, his advisors exchanged worried stares.

'As if the memorandum will change over a few hostages. We owe billions,' one said.

'And what is the price for a human's life these days?' a woman dressed in black asked and sat back in a high-back armchair.

'Even with VAT and inflation, it surely isn't a billion, that's for sure,' the short man with the thick mustache replied.

Relative time rushed again. Each passing minute brought a series of dead-ends to the ears of the prime minister. Disappointment filled the room until the police chief raised his phone to his ear after discreetly answering it.

'I'm in the prime minister's office. Talk quick,' his rough voice said, giving a shot at whispering.

The prime minister watched as his old friend's silvery mustache moved upwards, slightly above the corners of the chief's lips. The chief hardly smiled.

'Aha, okay, cut the tech gibberish and cut to the point. Do we have him? Hmm, okay, yeah, pick the suspect up and have him questioned. I'll be on my way back,' the chief continued, pretending to be unaware of the prime minister's eyes locked on him.

As the chief lowered his phone and his thumb press the red button to end the call, the prime minister stood up. 'Well?' was all he asked.

The tip of the chief's tongue watered his dry lips before he spoke. 'A kid in the tech lab found certain points or whatever they are called in the broadcasted voice and has been running them through a new system and comparing them with other recorded voices. A long shot. To be honest, no one was really expecting any results...'

'But?'

'He thinks he has a match...'

'Has he been arrested?'

'Units are on the way as we speak.'

Chapter 23

'What's that noise?' Jocasta asked as she leaped out of bed. For a split second, she had forgotten her whereabouts and was secretly enjoying Eugene's eyes fixed on her semi-covered figure.

'Gas,' he replied as he looked up to the built-in air-conditioning vents.

A cloud of reddish smoke invaded the room and with the doors and windows sealed shut; it did not take long to occupy every ounce of air that lingered in the bedroom.

Eugene picked up a small Zeus statue and ran to the door. He began to manically bang the base of the sculpture against the door.

'They won't break!' Jocasta yelled as she curled up on the bed and covered her mouth and nose with the bed sheet.

'Just a crack will help,' he shouted back and kept on hitting.

The statue's base broke off and fell to the carpeted floor. Zeus followed, and Eugene came tumbling after. Jocasta's eyes opened wide as she witnessed him pass out. She began to cough, and the thin sheet was not able to protect her. She lost consciousness a minute after Eugene.

She had no idea how much time had passed. She awoke in pitch black darkness, her hands firmly tied behind her back.

Greece knew well how much time had passed as the clock came to a full line of zeros. Time was up, demands weren't met, and the next victim was up.

'My dear pensioners, do not give up hope. The fight has just started. And every fight, every war, has its fatalities. We have been punished enough. Now, we earn our revenge and receive what is rightfully ours. Two will die next. Jocasta, the public parasite, and Eugene, the producer of lies, will be executed next. Mister prime minister, we mean business. Their blood is on your filthy hands. Watch as they die and know... you have three hours to announce a series of relief acts with immediate effect. No more promises. No more lies. Greece wants to hear what you have to offer without needing foreign approval. Last time I checked, we were still a free country. The land that gave birth to democracy cannot be a colony, mister unworthy prime minister. Announce what can be done, here and now. Enjoy the show.'

A green light spread throughout the room and Greece viewed Jocasta as she struggled to wake, having inhaled too much sleeping gas. Her eyes opened and closed a few times before being able to focus. As her vision cleared, she let out an echoing scream.

Eugene stood before her, just feet away. He was naked, still knocked-out and was tied to a wooden pole. A metal device had been placed around his head. Four long fishing lines were sewed into his lips and were connected to the strange helmet. Jocasta could not believe the mutilated, bloody lips were the same that were kissing her just hours ago. Just then, it occurred to her to look down at her own body. She was also naked, standing in an empty, tall glass pool.

Her scream must have woken Eugene up as he also seemed to be struggling to regain consciousness. Soon both locked eyes, yet remained silent. Jocasta shivered as she felt water at her feet. Since a child, she had feared the sea, the idea of drowning taunting most of her nightmares. A fear that she carried with her to adult life. Her pupils moved around, noticing that the glass cylinder's height only came to just above her breasts. Water was on the rise, and her breathing became heavier and turned into panting.

'You know, last night...' Eugene began to say.

'Don't... no need...'

'I just want you to know that you aren't a bad person. We are human and have our weaknesses and...' he said and turned towards the camera in the corner, 'this sick fuck,' he screamed, 'is a vicious bastard satisfying his perverted fantasies and shame on everyone who has been voting. Jocasta is a beautiful person, inside and out, and you lot just sit there. Sit there and watch her die, you sick cunts!'

Eugene was not known to swear. Everyone who knew him, watching on through their TV screens, could tell that he was petrified. And his worse phobia was yet to make an appearance.

'So, I skipped a few days off work, so what? Do I deserve to die? Please, please stop this madness,' Jocasta pleaded for her life as the water ceased flowing, her glass prison filled to the top. 'Your scapegoat for all the wrong doings of the public sector? They are over half a million public workers, come on! You believe you're punishing them by killing me? Let me go, please. I am not a criminal. I promise as soon as I leave this island, I will quit. I swear, I will. Please, please...'

As tears escaped her sore, reddish, drugged eyes, panic spread through government agencies and the metropolitan police.

'She said island!' one yelled from behind his computer.

'The place looks like a hotel, and that's where they thought they were heading. Get local police to check every hotel on an island that is listed as abandoned, under reconstruction or is closed for the winter period,' I said as I stood beside Captain Tito, in charge of the command center. I lowered my voice and looked him in the eyes. 'Sorry, Tito. Did not mean to step on your turf. It's just that Alexandro and Valentina...'

'No need for excuses,' his rough voice replied. 'Good idea, by the way. Though there are hundreds of hotels closed for the winter.'

Eugene's voice was heard and brought silence to the command room. We all turned our attention back to our screens.

'Stop begging him, Jocasta. He does not care about the people or Greece. He just wanted an excuse to torture and execute innocent people. I never raped anyone...'

'Lies!' the voice yelled, and a chilling, cold laughter followed. 'Greece has spoken. May you burn in eternal pain.'

Giant, slimy leeches started to come through the water pipe and into the pool holding Jocasta.

'Suck off the government? Tax payer's hard-earned cash? Let's see how you deal with your own kind, you leech!'

Jocasta screamed as the first leeches attached themselves to her feet. Crimson clouds of blood swam in the clear waters, causing the leeches to go into a frenzy. Dozens kept on coming out of the pipe.

Jocasta shrieked and shook all over. Eugene closed his eyes and lowered his head. He felt his empty stomach retaliating at the sight. Soon, he spat out yellowy, viscid saliva. There was nothing to throw up.

Multiple red circles appeared all over Jocasta's body as the deadly leeches used their sharp, tiny teeth to attach themselves to their host. Their heads disappeared under her skin while their snakish tails wiggled in the red waters. Soon, her body was fully covered with the minacious, vicious beasts. More daring leeches began to leap out of the water and attack her throat. One even made it as high as her cheek. Jocasta bit down on her lip hard and lines of blood formed in front of her teeth. She felt weak and dizzy. She closed her eyes. They never reopened again. She tried to think of happy thoughts and sought to reason with her inner inhibition as to whether she led the life she wanted. Her mind, though, went numb, unable to function under the torment. She drifted away and left her last breath, her mind thinking one last thought of regret. She never did become a mother.

'Next!'

Eugene braced himself and swallowed the lump gathering in his throat. 'Mama, I love you. You raised a good lad. Everything I am, is because of you,' he said, and a single tear ran down his icy cheek, dying upon his trembling lips.

His mother, who had been crying hysterically before the TV, refusing to leave the room as relatives tried to persuade her, silenced. 'My dear boy,' she whispered and touched the screen. The boy she held so many nights in her arms, the boy that would only sleep when she caressed his hair, her only child was about to be killed, and she was unable to do anything about it. She stroked the TV, imagining her old fingers running through his hair and then, she let out a wild scream, chilling all in the room. She stood up, straightened her flowery dress and ran for the apartment window. Relatives gasped as her sister jumped and knocked her to the ground, just feet away from the open window of the sixth floor.

A mechanical sound screeched, and Eugene cried out in pain. The hooks in his lips pulled his mouth wide open.

'We *ate* your words for years, mister. Your lies. Enjoy your last meal.'

A shower of bugs fell upon him. Hundreds of cockroaches, poisonous scorpions, red ants and various spiders covered his naked body. Eugene's arachnophobia kicked in as he felt multiple, pencil-thin legs tapping his naked body. He violently rocked back and forth, but his ties did not allow for much movement. Not enough to shake off his invaders. His eyes –in pure shock- shot from side to side as he felt insects moving upon his face. Instinctively, his brain gave the order to his mouth to close. His lips only moved a quarter of a centimeter and the wire began to rip through his skin. He yelled out in pain. A strange sound. A scream born in the throat. Produced without lips to make it sound human. A cockroach approached with caution and wandered on his bloody lips. A tiny fire ant also came close and was the first to enter his mouth.

Most viewers turned away in disgust. Over the years, Hollywood has brought our deepest, darkest nightmares to the big screen. Aliens, sharks, serial killers, ghosts, spiders. All there in our faces, yet fake. In the back of our mind, safety lingered, making us laugh off the jumps offered by the movie. Now, it was live. Raw and real in front of us. Not many could take it. Not many watched the entire twenty minutes of Eugene's ordeal. No single creature had enough poison to kill him. Yet, the combination of venom from four Indian scorpions, two black widows and hundreds of fire ants caused a chain reaction in his organs.

The longest of Hotel Murder's executions, the notorious heart rate line came to our screens as a relief. It flat-lined and signalled Eugene's tragic and gruesome passing.

Chapter 24

There is a certain charm about old Athenian neighborhoods. One could even go as far as saying they had a magical aura surrounding them. Tucked away in corners in the manic metropolis lay quiet streets with aging, yet well-maintained houses; their rich front lawns revealing that hard-working, senior Greek ladies resided there. Grandmas, most dressed in black, taking care of their gardens, painting their fences, picking fruit from trees and cooking delicious Greek food, using secrets carried through the centuries. Living history. Their manners, their way of thinking, their stories.

Mrs. Minoa was one such proud sixty-plus-year-old, living in one of Athens very first 'built-up' neighborhoods, living in the house her grandpa built after the war of 1922.

A widow, she dedicated most of her time to pampering her single son who still lived at home. Mrs. Minoa had her silver hair tied up in a clumsy bun and was busy washing the dishes by hand as she sang along to Haris Alexiou. Little did she notice the men in black exiting the vans opposite her house. More officers had entered her back garden and crept among the hand-painted gnomes. Soon, her home was surrounded.

Mrs. Voula Minoa placed the wet plate on the kitchen counter and wiped her hands on her new apron as she heard the stiff, loud knocking coming from her front door.

'Helen's early today,' she mumbled, her eyebrows signalling her annoyance. 'First chores, then coffee,' she continued as she thought of her gossip-loving friend, who she presumed was at her door.

'Coming,' she said much louder, knowing full well that stubborn Helen refused to wear her hearing aid. 'Ruins her look, she said,' Mrs. Minoa whispered and chuckled.

She grabbed the handle and pulled back the front door. 'Finished already, Helen?' she began to ask, before letting out a rough scream. The swat team was ready to break down her wooden door, and gun-wielding men rushed into her home, pushing her back upon the wall.

'Stay still, ma'am,' she was ordered by the tallest lady she had ever seen. 'Who else is in the house?' the woman continued as the police scattered around her home.

Mrs. Minoa could not utter a word. Her eyes opened wide and she trembled all over.

'Where is your son, Mrs. Minoa?' the officer asked louder.

Mrs. Minoa exhaled deeply and placed her hand upon her beating heart. 'My Lord, thank God I haven't mopped yet,' she finally spoke, her eyes watching the task force search around, shouting 'clear' to each other. 'My son is away on holiday for the week. What is all this commotion about?'

The task force officers stopped and lifted their dark helmet shades. None spoke to her. The tallest of them walked to the corner of the cozy-looking living room and spoke into his helmet's microphone. 'Sir? This is Swat11. The house and surroundings are clear. Aristoteli Minoa is not here, sir. Just his mother.'

'Goddamit,' Captain Savva's voice replied. 'I thought our sources confirmed him to be home.'

Captain Savva sat in the safety of a well-covered mini van, parked further down the street. He grabbed his ear set and pulled it over his blond hair, dropping the piece on the ground. 'Shit,' he whispered from behind closed teeth and stepped out of the black van, into the shade provided by the majestic oak trees that ran along the road. 'Pull the men out,' he ordered his silent partner by the van's monitor and began to stomp up to the house.

Captain Savva nodded back to swat officers exiting the premises as he covered the distance from the yellow-painted gate to the freshly-polished, wooden front door.

He knocked. Out of politeness, out of habit. He did not even know. Yet, he knocked and without waiting for a reply, he entered the house. Mrs. Minoa sat quietly in the center of her beige sofa. She raised her head towards the handsome man before her and followed him with her eyes to the worn-in armchair opposite her.

'Mrs. Minoa,' he said, 'I am police Captain Savva. Paul Savva. As you have been informed, we are here looking for your son, Aristoteli. The theatre where he works told us that he is at home, sick. Took a three day leave, they said.'

'Did he now?' she replied, her hands stroking her knees, rubbing her dirty apron.

'You did not know?'

She closed her eyes and took in a deep breath. 'Boys don't always tell the whole truth to their mothers, do they now?' she asked and a strange smile appeared on her aging face. 'He said he took a few days off to go on a cruise. A well-deserved weekend getaway, that's how he put it.'

'Which cruise? To where? Alone?' Captain Savva shot three questions at her.

She shrugged her shoulders. 'I presumed with friends and hoped for a lady friend, to be honest. Destination? I do not know. One of the cruises from Piraeus,' she said and stood up. 'Where are my manners? Coffee, Captain?'

'Sit down, ma'am,' Captain Savva said with a heavy, loud voice.

Mrs. Voula Minoa obeyed and with shocked eyes, landed straight back down on the comfortable couch. 'No need to yell, young man. I have done nothing wrong. Sorry, I cannot help you more. This is all I know. I deserve, no I demand, better treatment.'

'All you know, huh?' he replied. 'I see where your son gets his acting skills from. Not once have you inquired as to why we are searching for your son. I believe you know that your son is up to no good. Consider yourself under house arrest until I speak with a judge. Maybe a walk out of your front door in hand-cuffs for all your friends to see will refresh your memory.'

Mrs. Minoa did not reply. She sat in silence as the Captain stood up and went to the front door to call in a pair of officers to keep an eye on her. Mrs. Voula Minoa quickly pulled out her cell phone from the apron's lone pocket. With trembling hands, she managed to text faster than she had ever done before.

'THE POLICE ARE HERE. THEY KNOW ABOUT ARISTOTELI.'

Maintaining her cool, she slid the device back into her pocket and leaned back into the leather sofa. She closed her eyes and pictured the boss receiving her text. He would surely get angry, yet the boss always had a plan. That man's brain fascinated her. *Yes, yes. He surely has a plan. My boy will be safe and Greece will be reborn*, she thought, and a sinister smile rested on her pale face.

Miles away, her text took just a second to cross the sea and force the boss's phone to beep.

The tall man took his phone into his hand and looked down at the message feeling glad the signal was not blocked in the control room. He ground his teeth and clenched his left hand into a fist. A man of few words and many plans, he ordered, 'Set in motion the prison break!'

*****

I also was on my way to meet a Greek mother.

A break of sorts did come to my case. Ioli was right as she was most of the time. I remembered the night we drove onto that run down street. She felt a familiarity around the deteriorating houses. I must admit, her words ran through my mind on a rainy, sleepless night and my gut persuaded me that the road meant something to me too.

Turns out, it meant something to us all.

Soon, SERENITY nursing home filled my horizon. A three-storey, mid-century, dull beige building with a large, bright green front lawn took up the entire street opposite me. I illegally parked in a 'taxis-only' square and quickly hopped out my Audi, hoping no menacing taxi-driver eyes saw me. If anyone can curse, it's Greeks. You can imagine the tongue on our professional drivers.

The busy street showed no signs of an empty parking spot and I was on official business. That was my excuse, and I was sticking to it.

I sprinted across, avoiding traffic, or better yet, traffic was avoiding me. The sound of an angry horn escorted me to the sidewalk. The new born, shamrock-green grass was luring me to take off my shoes and walk upon it. To head to the nearest tree, lay down and escape reality. One of the things I missed about being a father was the days at the park. To carelessly relax, drift away from the polluted city and sit in nature, enjoying my baby girl playing around.

I knelt and gently caressed the tips of the waving grass. 'Not today, my friend. Not today.'

The building managed to seem in a decent state; to fool visitors of its well-being. However, a closer eye would reveal many cracks in the wall; chipped, sloppy patches of paint ran along the wall and the wooden window frames begged for some loving maintenance.

My knees whined about the fifteen steps up to the main entrance. The building was not built as a last home for seniors dropped off by their families –if they were lucky enough as to have a family that is. These massive buildings were government buildings built during prosperity ages, decades ago. Now, they had become retirement homes, dumping grounds for filing purposes and if lucky, libraries or museums of sorts. If unlucky, they were abandoned to the elements to devour. Something like the Olympic Village from the 2004 games that sank in an ocean of stubborn weeds and bushes.

Fifteen. I counted the steps in an effort to please my aching knees that the top was not so far away.

I stood before the locked, tall door and caught my breath. My index finger obeyed the written instructions and pushed the buzzer. A prolonged *ding-dong* echoed in the hollow, vast welcoming area inside.

No voice came from the speaker inquiring who I was or what I wanted.

Visitor hours had already begun. The door opened on its own, having been buzzed opened by the young brunette in the white nurse uniform standing behind the reception booth.

'Come in, sir,' she said. 'Who are you visiting today?' she asked, her eyes looking down at her chart.

'Antigoni Lemoni.'

'Very well. Sign here, sir. Mrs. Antigone is in the back yard in the picnic area,' she said, and her palm pointed to the large patio doors behind her, to the right. 'Members of staff will help you if you need anything,' she added, checking my signature. 'Have a nice day, sir.'

I smiled back at her and sauntered upon the chlorine-smelling tiled floor to the back and exited to the vast green area hidden behind the building. I got Alice in Wonderland vibes as the oasis of palm trees, clear-water lake with playful ducklings, picnic tables, and mini-golf course welcomed me. The cement jungle of Athens seemed miles away. A world of vivid greens and a rainbow of flowers unfolded, and if it were not for the dozens of sickly-looking elders, it would have been a heavenly image.

Most relatives walk straight up to their grandfather or grandmother, having enjoyed the view and facilities upon their first visit. This I guessed as I was the only one standing by the patio doors. A bald man in his early forties in a shirt a bit too small for his body, with the SERENITY logo printed upon it, came to my side.

'Can't find your loved one?' he asked in a voice that revealed a man trying to cope with a cold.

The kind man listened to me and asked me to follow him. Soon, I sat beside the old lady, dressed in pitch black clothes from top to bottom. Even her pure white hair was caged in a black see-through hairnet.

Even though her story was a tragic one, the winter sun, the surroundings and the strong Greek coffee made the next half an hour pass by rather enjoyably.

Leaving the nursing home, I felt more puzzled than before. My dead billionaire case was on life support, with me electroshocking it back to life.

If only Ioli had picked up her phone at that very moment. Maybe, things would have played out differently. Maybe, people now deceased would still be breathing under the sun.

But, as I held my cell phone to my ear all I heard was multiple beeps followed by Ioli's voice message.

Chapter 25

Funny how we all remember the exact moment and location when Lady Tragedy strikes.

Ioli was already having a *bad day*. Two words we say to cover all the crap we can't be bothered to number.

A careless run-in with the corner of the kitchen table, offering a fine, round, purple bruise.

A late night argument with Mark about things that seemed insignificant an hour later.

Her monthly period deciding to arrive early and with force.

A infant son crying through the night due to fever.

A dent and a scratch on her beloved car. Ioli reversed; the trash can came forward.

Driving to work, having to deal with Athens' infamous morning traffic jams while drinking your second coffee, wishing for its magical powers to help with your 'lack of sleep', menacing migraine.

A bad day by definition.

Ioli didn't manage to get much done during her first hour at the office. Her back and her head competed to see who could cause her more discomfort.

She stood up, opened her desk drawer and took out two painkillers. The little white pills sat on the tip of her tongue as she raised her green tea to her lips. She then took out a maxi pad from the bottom drawer and headed to the bathroom.

As she sat down on the cold toilet seat, her phone vibrated in the right pocket of her navy blue jeans.

'Babe, I'm sorry. Love, Dr. Jackass,' she read Mark's message. As her finger began to type a reply, she heard Koula call out to her.

'Ioli, you there?'

'Yes, Koula. I'll be out in five,' Ioli replied, failing to hide the annoyance in her voice.

'Where's your pager? There have been multiple breakouts from Korydallos prison, and there's an on-going uprising. It's chaotic. Wardens have asked for police and army backup. We have been teamed up. Me, you, Adam and Nick. Car 17, down in the parking. We are waiting for you.'

Boy, can Koula talk fast.

'On my way.'

Fucking wicked day, more like it.

It was as her wet hand grabbed the door-knob that the thought ran through her tired mind. Shivers travelled down her spine and her heart changed its rhythmic pace. 'The Olympus killer,' she said.

Her first big case. The maniac who wished her dead. The idea of him being loose frightened an otherwise fearless Cara. Her mind thinking only of Icarus, her son.

She took out her phone and called Mark. He answered straight away.

'Hey, glad you called. Was thinking 'bout last night and...'

'Mark, listen to me,' she said, her tone scaring him to silence.

'What's wrong?'

'Have you left home yet?'

'No. On my way now.'

'Cancel your shift. Don't take Icarus to the babysitter. Stay with him and head out of town. A fun day trip...'

'Babe, slow down. What's happening?'

'I'm running down the stairs. We have been called to Korydallos prison. There's an uprising, and many inmates have escaped...'

'The Olympus killer?'

'Maybe. Please...'

'Don't stress. I will take him to see my mother in the village. Don't worry about us, but for the love of God, please be careful. Don't be the hero. Let someone else deal with...'

'Love you. Talk later,' Ioli said and jumped in the back of the police vehicle waiting for her.

Korydallos was Greece's major prison. The only one accommodating offenders serving life sentences. It's tall, monotonous-beige walls hid appalling conditions for those enclosed inside. Outsiders judged the lack of European standards, yet the average Greek was glad to have the 'animals' thrown in a 'cage'.

'It's a prison, not a hotel,' my grandmother used to say.

Like all days, the prison's daily routine began at six o'clock sharp, with no signs of how the next hours would play out.

The sinister voice took over the prison system as inmates were in the back-yard for their 'free hour' of the day. Some were in detention, others in the one-room library, others showering.

'Attention, all inmates. Your help is needed to help Greece rise from its ashes. It is time you were freed,' the distorted voice said, gaining their attention. The few guards –less than years gone by due to cutbacks- exchanged worried stares. Loud bangs echoed through the halls and around the building. All doors, even the outer gates opened. As though someone had pressed all release buttons on the control board.

'Shit! Technology is always against us,' a warden with thick hazelnut hair said to his partner.

'The armor room is also open, my friends,' the voice continued. 'Take back your freedom,' it said louder. 'Rise, my brothers, rise!'

It took a minute or so for the surreal scenario to sink in. One by one, the inmates cheered and ran for the front gates. Others ran inside in search of guns. Others to the nearest phone to call their associates on the outside.

Wardens fired warning shots that were ignored.

'Shoot at their feet,' an officer commanded. 'If needed... a bullet to the leg.'

Chaos.

Total chaos.

Soon, inmates fell dead by the front gate, wardens were murdered and multiple fires broke out.

Panic in the nearby neighborhoods spread like a new-born spark of fire playing in a pile of hay.

Forty-three minutes after the voice's announcement, Ioli arrived at the prison. All officers were provided with Kevlar helmets, an earpiece to listen to the commander of the operation, and a bulletproof vest.

'Do we know which prisoners have escaped and which are still inside?' Ioli asked.

'No, not yet,' a fellow officer replied. 'We can't be sure of anything as we are unable to enter various sections. Wardens and other prison personnel are being held hostage. Inmates have already sent out demands for better conditions. Others are on a murder spree.

Either killing inmates of different clans or taking revenge on personnel. The prison doctor was thrown out the window of the third floor... he was missing an arm.'

One by one, the police officers listened to the plan, to their orders and entered the prison. Ioli knew well where she would be heading. Second floor, cell 52. The Olympus Killer.

Most of the police force was deployed around the surrounding neighborhoods and roadblocks by the army formed a ring around the prison. One by one, escaped inmates fell dead if they resisted capture. Most raised their hands in the air, obeyed when ordered to drop their weapons and lay on the ground.

Inside the prison, things were trickier. Gang mentality did not allow willing inmates be surrounded. In groups, they fought against law enforcement officers, both sides suffering fatalities.

Ioli crept past burnings officers and dumpsters releasing black smoke. Deafening gunfire bounced around the tall walls covering the yelling by all involved in the hellish day. Ioli ran up the metal stairway to the second floor, her gun faithfully by her side.

Empty cells welcomed her. No one -seemingly- remained on the upper floors of the cockroach-infested establishment. Her breath stopped, lingering in her open mouth. She was just a cell away. She raised her firearm and leaped in front of the open cell bars.

A half-naked body lay on the dirty floor. Blood all over. A screwdriver decorated with thick blood by the stabbed prisoner. The word ARES written in blood on the cracked mirror above the moldy sink.

He killed him on the first chance he got. He will never change.

Suddenly, a hand fell upon her gun, trying to pull it away from her. Another hand slithered around her neck.

'My Athena!'

Every hair and pore on her skin stood up. That familiar demonic hiss of his voice. His twisted, perverted mind still set on murdering the ancient Olympian gods. Ioli bowed and bit his arm with force, escaping his tight hold.

'Ooh,' he said, and his green eyes opened with excitement. 'Just like old times,' he said and licked his lips.

Ioli kicked backwards, hitting him right between his thighs. He yelled in pain, let go of her gun and took a step back.

'Is that any way to treat an old friend? I know you have missed me, my sweet honey ball of rage.'

Ioli stood her ground opposite him, raising her gun towards him. He looked different. He had shaved away his rich hair, a long, untamed beard hung from his skinny face, and he looked unhealthy, dirty, sickly. Yet, the evil smirk was still there. That flash of passion in his eyes; passion for killing.

'I never did get the chance to kill you,' she said.

He laughed hysterically and mocked the word. 'Kill? Me? I made you!'

'Attack me,' Ioli said, a cool, calm tone travelling with the words.

'What?'

'Attack me,' she repeated, kicking the screwdriver in his direction. 'Athena is still on your list.'

The notorious Olympus Killer laughed again. He shook his head and knelt to pick up the bloody tool. He stood up straight and lifted it, ready to throw it over the rails.

'Judge, I thought he was coming at me.'

'What? What are you on about? And they call me crazy,' he said, waving the long screwdriver at her.

One shot.

One shot between the eyes.

That's all it took. And she was finally free. Free from the only demon she had ever met.

She never needed to use her rehearsed line in a court of law. Among the forty-seven bodies belonging to inmates that day, he was just a number. No one questioned her report.

Evil was out of her life for good.

Order was restored, and two hours later, Ioli was back at headquarters. As she picked up the phone to call Mark, she noticed my missed call and called me back as I was driving away from SERENITY.

Who would have believed that after her retelling of her day that it was my words that would shock her?

'The old lady called him what?'

Chapter 26

Valentina sat on the ground, her feet close to her body, her head upon her knees and her hands covering her ears. They listened as Jocasta and Eugene screamed and suffered, loud and clear through the hotel's sound system. Each room equipped with cameras, microphones and speakers. Alexandro had tried to stop the sound, his heart breaking at Valentina's obvious agony. The built-in speaker taunted them from the ceiling above. Alexandro pushed one of the armchairs below it and tried to reach it by standing on the chair's tall back. Twice he fell before giving up and going next to Valentina, stroking her hair. As she cried, he stood back up and threw books to the relentless speaker above them. Nothing stopped Eugene's cries from piercing their ears.

Apollo, too, kept himself busy. He seemed preoccupied with the marble fireplace.

'It's blocked,' Alexandro said as he stood on the armchair. 'Sealed like everything in this fucking room.'

Apollo nodded and continued to inspect the walls. As Alexandro gave up with his book tossing and sat beside Valentina, Apollo began to move around the various ornaments on the mantel shelf.

With the final beep of the digital heart-beat, a short-lived silence spread in the library. Short-lived as a loud, earth-shaking sound made Valentina and Alexandro to look up towards Apollo.

Apollo stood in amazement as the entire fireplace began to move clockwise, revealing a passage behind it.

'I knew it,' he announced, beaming and raising his fist into the air.

'What is that?' Elias asked in the next room, placing his ear on the cool white wall. 'Like someone moving around large rocks.'

'Bastards get... getting their next kill... kill... killing device ready. Are we... hmm... next?' his brother Dinos replied, his childhood stutter returning. 'Well, there go, goes years of therapy... down the... the... the drain!'

'Just relax,' Clio said, placing her hand on his shoulder. *Easier said than done,* she thought and then spoke. 'Maybe, it's one of the guests. Maybe we should yell for help?'

'And, if it's not them? If it's our killers?' Elias asked, his palms and right ear still upon the wall.

'They are planning on killing us anyway, right? What have we got to lose?' Clio replied.

The triplets exchanged a meaningful stare, before beginning to scream for help and banging on the wall. The loud sound had died out, yet no reply ever came.

'This is hopeless,' Dinos said and sat down on the floor.

'This is hopeless,' Diana also said as she opened all the kitchen cupboards and checked for food or anything helpful towards an escape. 'Out of all the places, I get stuck in a food-less kitchen. Well, screw my freaking luck, hey?'

Below her, in one of the many basements of the vast building, Maximos had just woken up. An insomniac since his rebellious teen years, the sleeping gas offered his body a chance to rest.

His eyes opened in the dim-lighted room. He was lying down, unable to get up. As he wiggled his body, he felt and heard chains move and rattle.

'At least I'm horizontal. My feet have been killing me,' he joked.

Jokes were always his safe place. Scruffy-looking since childhood with manly features, most expected him to be the Alpha type, rough, Greek villager and Maximos stepped right into the shoes society made for him. Yet, deep down a gentle soul rested. A soul that enjoyed fine art, French cuisine and classical music. Aspects even close friends did not know about. Maximos played the part of the macho, cursing farmer well.

'I've had a good life,' he whispered. Words destined for the comfort of his own ears. He had many regrets. Regrets he was not willing to admit, even to himself. His uproarious laughter followed. 'Damn right, I had a good life,' he said louder.

The darkness did not reply.

Maximos started to study the ceiling. Counting the cracks. Watching a fat moth being lured to the two faint light bulbs. He moved around his broad shoulders and listened to them crack. His mind travelled to Ramona, the olive-skinned Spanish lady that ran the beauty parlor at the end of his street. He paid her well, for her massages. Every Sunday at twelve. The only day he did not work. After church, he would swim for an hour in his near Olympic-dimension-sized swimming pool, shower and then enjoy her gentle, expert hands.

He was not sure how long had passed since he had awoken, but he was certain that he was bored. Bored of the room, and bored of his thoughts.

'Excuse me,' he called out. 'Mister sicko with the robot voice?' he asked, raising his voice. 'I'm bored. Can we get this over and done with?'

Silence.

'Pretty please?' he mocked.

Still no reply.

'Oh, come on, dude. What's your plan? Bore me to death? I'm hungry and need to shit like a constipated cow given laxatives. If you are not killing me now, untie me. Play some music. Say something I'm giving up on you!'

With that lyric in mind, Maximos spent the next fifty minutes singing and talking to himself. A restless spirit, being tied down was torture enough. If he only knew what the future held for him, maybe he wouldn't be in such a rush to be executed.

'Good afternoon, Greece. It is with joy that certain demands have been met. I am sure as this is a matter of life and death, you have all been keeping up with the on-going news. The prime minister's speech and the new measures announced satisfy us. Yet, more needs to be done in the right direction. Our major demands, known from the beginning, have not been met. We are not irrational. We will not be unreasonable. No one will be executed as steps were made in the right direction. We are fighting for the Greeks and their survival. No more demands will be made. You have all day to announce the passing laws. Laws that will satisfy all demands made by us so far. If not, the first criminal will be executed in two hours. Then the next and the next. Every two hours. Until none are left, and their blood will be on your hands, Mister Prime-Minister.'

Maximos rolled his eyes. 'Great, another two hours stuck here.'

'Two hours in the prison of my mind, prison of my mind. Two whole hours... la la la la,' he sang as he banged his head on the steel plate he lay on.

'Time is on my side, yes, it is...' he continued with his favorite band, The Rolling Stones. A smile came to life as he remembered travelling to London for their concert.

Was it 1983 or 84? he thought. *It was a once in a lifetime experience, that's for sure.*

Inevitably, his mind thought of his trip's companion. His ex-wife, Rena.

'No, Maximos. Don't go down that street,' he whispered. The love of his life, he did her wrong way too many times. A fan of the booze and the so-called weaker sex, Maximos was not made out for marriage. Three kids followed, two hated him while his youngest daughter put up with him, mostly to enjoy his expensive gifts. It had been three years since he had last spoken to Rena. A typical conversation over the phone. She asked for a raise in child support, and he replied with a casual, 'Fine, no problem.'

Money came easy to Maximos, if not always in a completely legal way.

'It's just bending the rules,' he would say, and it was his motto not only to his farming business but to life.

Two hours came, ruled and evanesced.

The image of tied-up Maximos on what seemed to be a metal runway, like those used in factories to move products around, appeared on screens around the country.

'Nexttodie votes have passed the one hundred thousand mark. Congratulations, Greece. As always, your wishes are my command. The leech of sponsored funds has been chosen. The multimillionaire farmer with the extravagant life, Maximos is next to pay for his sins. Sins made on our backs with our tax money...'

'Fuck you, man. I worked hard,' Maximos shouted and brought a sad smile upon the faces of those who knew him. They all knew his sins, they all knew he did not work hard for his vast fortune. Now, they were about to witness his death.

'... As a farmer, you must know what a combine harvester is.'

And with that, a loud noise spread out in the low-ceilinged basement. Maximos began to move backwards. More lights pushed shadows back into their corners and Maximos leaned his head back to see where his destination would be. A long, red harvester –the type he owned many of, his favorites to collect wheat- spun round just feet away from him. Upon it shiny, sharp blades had been added.

'Mince-meat it is,' he joked.

'Rena,' he yelled. 'Rena, my love. I'm sorry. You deserved better. I truly, truly loved you. All those whores meant nothing, my queen. Vasili, Sergio, Polina, you are the best things that I ever planted. Live your lives to the fullest,' he said as he felt the wind from the machine blowing on his hair.

'*One last song,*' he thought and began to sing the chorus from Frank Sinatra's anthem. 'I did it my way...' were the last words that came out of Maximos's loud, foul-mouth lips. He did not scream, though the pain was excruciating. His body shook as it was eaten up by the machinery. Blood spatter covered the machine, and body tissue was flung into the air as Maximos was ground into pieces.

As the last, prolonged beep representing his heart silenced, the voice came back.

'Two hours.'

Chapter 27

'There's nearly no one left!' Elias cried as Maximos was executed. 'Think of the group. Who's left? Shit, we are next. I feel it. All this because our parents are rich and we posted a few photos on Instagram. Fuuuuck!'

His brother, Dinos, walked up and down the room behind him, biting his nails.

'Not that I wish bad on anyone, but there is still that sexy lady who owns Humbo, the gentleman with the name of a Greek god and the two cops,' Clio said calmly as she stood in the corner of the room, her head leaned back on the wall and her eyes closed. 'Wow, you two are right. I am bad with names.'

'Diana, Apollo, Alexandro and, and, and Valentina. And you're forgetting the bi... bishop's wife, Salome,' Dinos said.

'Your memory never ceases to amaze me. We only really heard all their names during the listing of our *crimes*,' Clio said, sarcasm enwrapping the last word. 'If they murdered the Bishop alone, I doubt they will kill his wife from now on.'

'Yes, because *they* have shown such a kind heart so far, right?' Elias snapped.

Clio exhaled and opened her eyes. 'Well, she wasn't on the blame list, was she?'

'Cops weren't either,' Dinos commented.

'The group of ladies was certain that the cops were actors.'

'Which means, Clio, we are, at most, three kills away from being slaughtered,' Elias said, breathing heavily, his fingers grouped together into tight fists.

Clio looked around the bare room. The walls seemed so close. She watched her brothers and thought, *At least, we are together.*

She slid down the wall and sat on the hard ground. She fought back tears as she realized that maybe she would witness her brothers die. Just then she thought of her poor parents. They had tried for years to have children without success. After countless of fruitless procedures, one day the gynecologist announced to her mother, that not only was she finally pregnant, but she was carrying triplets. Not a single soul on the planet was happier that day than her parents. And now, they were going to watch all three of them perish before their eyes.

'We have to get out of here,' she said, her throat clogged up.

'No shit, Sherlock. How?'

Clio looked up at the cameras. Both with a red light. She was sure they were switched off and came on during their executions.

'We first have to die.'

Both brothers stared at their sister. What was brewing in her mind?

Rooms away, Diana gave up searching the room for food or anything she could use. She had hoped for a knife. She pictured herself stabbing her attacker. She always toyed with the idea of being the hero. Her grandfather's war stories and the praise he received were idolized by her as a child.

A cheese-less mouse-trap, a dirty plunger, a bottle of expired dishwasher liquid and a small box of rat poison. Her plunder from her search. No knife.

I'll blind them with the dishwasher, hit them with the plunger and force feed them the poison.

She chuckled at the thought. Her eyes remained fixed on the rat poison. 'Could it work on humans?' she pondered as she knelt and picked up the old box. She turned the box around and tried to read the faded letters.

'Kills mice and rats... keep out of the reach of children... if accidentally swallowed, contact your doctor...'

Diana threw it back into the cupboard. 'Nope, I am not dying like a freaking rodent. Puking and aching and then it probably won't even work. Anyway, Nana always said Christians don't commit suicide. 'A high sin,' she said, imitating her grandma's shaky voice. 'A special place in hell, God has for them. You are not even buried in the cemetery. They throw you over the wall.'

Diana sat back down on the floor. 'This is the special hell, Nana.'

A click in the silence caught her attention. It came from behind the door. Diana placed her right hand on the floor and struggled to stand up. She controlled her breath and closed her eyes, ready for the worst. The door moved backwards and two hooded men, both with guns in their hands, entered the room. Diana had no time to react, no chance to be the hero as she desired. The chloroform-covered cloth settled on her mouth and nose. The tall man's strong hands holding it down. The other injected her with a see-through liquid and Diana felt like falling. An avid skydiver, she knew the feeling well. The entire earth far from your feet. A sense of drowning in one's mind and then, all goes blank.

Diana opened her drowsy eyes. It burned to fully open them, but she did not mind. Locked away in that kitchenette, she made peace with herself and swore to her inner, proud self that she would exit this world with her head held high. Though, fear conquered her heart on how she would leave this life. Just thinking of the previous deaths, made her backbone shiver and tremble. The dizziness of the drugs wore off gradually, and her ears heard the last words of the voice as he wished her a good death.

Viewers heard how three hundred and sixty-two workers lost their jobs in a day. Above Diana's head now hung a pot filled with liquid acid. Three hundred and sixty-two liters of it.

Diana waited for her sentence. She prayed it was not anything alive like bugs and rats. 'A decent way to die, God.'

The pot of sulfuric acid tilted and death rained from above.

A whole body melted in less than a minute. Skin popping and vanishing in seconds, hair frizzling up and bones left to rot in a red pool of blood. A human body turned into a bloody soda.

'Two hours, Prime Minister. Two hours. Tick tock, tick tock!'

Chapter 28

'It's pitch dark in here,' Valentina said as she grabbed onto Alexandro's hand and followed him into the cavernous hallway, her shadowy figure blending in with the blackness.

'It gets narrow after a few steps. I can't see a thing, but we can feel our way along the wall. Anywhere than back there,' Apollo's voice came from the darkness.

'Wait,' Valentina called out to him and stepped back out into the library. She searched around on the fireplace shelf and lifted up and teapot-looking ornament. 'Yes!'

'What is it, pumpkin?'

Valentina could not resist a smile. She resented the adjective – it wasn't the thinnest of fruit- yet as Alexandro used it so fondly, with a sweetness in his voice, it grew on her.

'Matches. A full box, too,' she answered, and with one worried look behind her, she stepped into the secret passageway. She lit the first match, and faint light fought back the darkness. The walls were made out of old bricks and the mud that once glued them together had begun to turn to dust. Deserted spider webs were spread out among the rocks while mold and mildew covered a large portion of the ground.

The short-lived flames frizzled and vanished. Valentina lit the next, and with an exchange of stares with Alexandro, they both scurried along. Match by match, the group of three moved along.

'What if this is a trap?'

'How could it be, Valentina? They have no idea we would guess that the fireplace moved?'

'Look at the flame. It's leaning forward; the wind is behind us. We could be heading to a dead end.'

'You worry too much,' Apollo said. 'It's a hidden hallway. It should be closed on both ends.'

Alexandro stroked her hand. 'We will find a way out,' he reassured her.

The passage took a curve to the right and soon, they came to an end. Valentina lit three matches at once for more light. A Hobbit-sized door stood closed before them.

'The key is on the door,' Alexandro said, and his eyes opened wide. He squeezed Valentina's hand and kissed her on the neck.

Apollo turned the key and pulled back the door by its huge round handle. The wooden door moaned as it was forced to move and scraped its way along the floor.

'Well, aren't we fucking lucky,' Apollo said as sunlight came rushing through. Waves crashing upon beach rocks and seagulls fighting over dead fish could be heard.

'We are on the beach,' Valentina said and ducked, peeping outside. No one was to be seen. From what she could tell from the windows above, they were at the back of the building. 'We have to be careful not to be seen.'

'And go where?' Alexandro said.

'We swim?' Apollo suggested.

'You mad?' Valentina snapped and then apologized. 'I mean, we have no idea how far we are from the next island or what direction to go.'

'No. I'm the one that's sorry,' he replied. 'You're right. It's just if we stay here, we're dead.'

'What about the ferry?' Alexandro asked, also ducking and looking outside. The blue sea had never been so beautiful before. He took a deep breath of fresh air and let the warm sun play around upon his cold face.

'If it's still here, it will be up front where we docked,' Valentina said and bit her lower lip.

'Don't darken your face. I promised you off this island, and off this God-forsaken rock we will go,' Alexandro said and took her into his arms.

Just then, a vibration was felt by both of them. Valentina looked down at her leg.

'Is that...'

'My phone!'

Alexandro pulled out his cell from his right pocket, its green light illuminating the dark surroundings. 'It's Ioli!'

'Unbelievable! You sure? Is it working?' Apollo said and came closer, staring at the phone.

'Hello? Oh, my God. Ioli! I can't believe it's you.'

Alexandro stepped back and bowed his head; his phone stuck to his ear. ' Yes, Valentina is here with me. Aha, hmm, yeah, okay...' he lowered his voice and took another step back.

'What's wrong?' Valentina asked, observing his eyes.

'Nothing,' he replied mumbling and avoiding eye contact. 'Great news! The police know where we are and are on their way.'

Valentina closed her eyes and whispered, 'Thank God.'

'So, we stay put?' Apollo asked. 'No need to risk going outside.'

Valentina opened her eyes and turned towards Alexandro. 'The triplets are still alive. They're just kids...'

'The police are on the way,' Apollo said.

'We are the police,' she replied, pointing to herself and Alexandro. 'And, time is almost up. With us gone, they will be next.'

'Babe, how? Go out and walk around the place? It's sealed off, and there are cameras everywhere.'

'Man has a point,' Apollo said, sitting down and leaning back against the wall.

'However, now you say, we cannot stay here.'

'Why not?' Apollo said, slightly raising his voice.

'If you are next, Apollo, that means that soon, men will come looking for you. In the library! And, guess what they will see? A passageway behind a fireplace.'

'Shit,' he said and quickly stood up, rubbing his lower back.

'Maybe, that's how we save the triplets. We go outside, find somewhere to hide. Let's hope Apollo is next. Sorry, Apollo.'

'No need,' he said, waving his hand. 'I get your point. If I am next, we gain time, with them looking for me. Let's hope the police arrive on time, before they find us or turn on the Afroudaki kids.'

The group of three carefully stepped out into the sun. With their backs against the wall, and their eyes tuned to alert mode, they made their way to the mansion's corner.

A row of bare hills ran along in the distance. Rocks and dried grass were all the hills housed. The hotel was the only building on the golden sandy beach.

'Did Ioli say where we are?'

'Pano Antikeri. A private island near Keros,' Alexandro said.

Apollo looked back at them. 'Pano, you said? Or Kato?' (*Pano=Up, *Kato=Down).

'Yeah, Pano. Why?'

'You sure?'

Alexandro squinted his eyes. 'What's wrong, Apollo?'

'Nothing, nothing,' he said, shaking his head. 'Erm, it's just that you said private island. Kato Antikeri is privately owned. Not Pano.'

Alexandro took a step towards him. 'That's some genius trivial knowledge you have there. You know every privately owned rock in these vast waters?'

'Hey,' Apollo said, placing his hand upon Alexandro's chest. 'I'm in the fishing industry and have a photographic memory. What's with the aggravation?'

Alexandro replied with a single, 'Nothing.'

Valentina took him by the hand and rubbed his fingers with hers. 'What's up?' she whispered.

'Nothing. Let's get to those hills. See there?' he asked pointed in the distance. Valentina nodded. 'Looks like a row of small caves. We'll hide out there until Ioli and the police arrive.

Both looked around and above at the sealed windows of the mansion. Without saying another word, they both dashed out into the sunlight, away from the dark shadows of Hotel Murder. Apollo swallowed the lump in his throat and stood still for a second or two. He watched them sprint for the caves. He placed one hand on the brick wall, scratched his hair with the other, whispered his favorite curse word and ran after them.

Chapter 29

The three men stood before their multiple monitors. Every inch of the mansion was being recorded. Many empty, dark rooms and a few rooms lit, featuring dead bodies.

They watched as Apollo, Valentina and Alexandro vanished into the dark cavity behind the 19th-century fireplace.

'Okay, they are on their way,' Platonas said, sitting in front of the screens' control monitor.

'What's going on there?' the forty-year-old man with the cat-like eyes asked, towering him from behind.

Their attention turned towards the man's hairy finger, tapping on the 5th screen on the 2nd row.

'Sound, please,' he said.

'On it, Dad,' Platonas said and pressed the orange button with the sound symbol.

'What are those triplets up to?'

In the round room, Clio and her brothers had no clue as to who was listening in.

The three stood in a small circle, close to each other and listened as Clio showed them her unlabeled nail vanish. 'I will pretend its poison,' she whispered as quietly as she could. 'I will go into anaphylactic shock. You will pretend that I'm dying. Let me die. When I stop moving, you two will argue about how it was Dinos's idea to come here and strangle each other. Do it by the door. By the side. When they come in and open the door, they will come straight for me, in the middle of the room. You two will get up and run. I will stay and play dead. As they chase you, I will follow. One of us should make it out, get some signal and call the police.'

'That's fucking dumb. It isn't going to work,' Elias said.

'Got a better idea?'

'No. But, when this is made into a movie, we are going to be that lame scene when the stupid kids made up a childish plan...'

'Shut up, Elia,' Dinos said. 'It's our only chance.'

Back in the control room, Platonas's dad rolled his eyes. 'Rich kids!'

Platonas chuckled. 'They are next to die anyway. Shall we just send in the men, now, before the whole parody charade begins?'

'No,' Aristoteli replied. 'I want to see how awful their acting is going to be. Great sound system by the way. Picking up whispers from that distance.'

'See, Dad? My studies did not go to waste.'

His father smiled and stepped forward to place his hand upon his son's shoulder. He was indeed proud of him. Yet, his hand remained in flight and did not land. His smiled flatlined, and his eyes turned towards the screen showing the south side of the building.

'Well, what's going on there? That cop doesn't look happy. Do we have sound from outside?

'No, Pop. But, we have sound from the bug under his collar. Give me a sec.'

Soon, the three men were listening to Alexandro saying that it was nothing.

'Is the recording saved somewhere?'

'It's on a half an hour loop,' Platonas replied, looking up at his father.

'Take it back to the moment where they entered the passage,' he ordered and sat down in the chair next to him. 'Let's see what we missed.'

Minutes later, all three men stared at each other in shock.

'How the hell is his phone working?' Aristoteli said, squinting his eyes, looking at Platonas sideways. 'You said you killed all cell phone signal on the island.'

'I did...'

'Maybe you set the timer wrong for it to go off,' his father said, calmer than Aristoteli.

'It's timed to go off *after* the triplets' execution,' Platonas said, raising his voice. 'I know my job.'

'Maybe your gadget doesn't work outside.'

'I tested it twice. Someone has killed our block...'

'Shh,' his father said and waved his hands. 'That cop is saying something.'

All three heard that the police were on the way.

Platonas and Aristoteli both turned towards their leader. Both waiting for his thoughts.

Their leader walked towards the wall and gently placed his head upon it. He closed his eyes and said, 'Forget the triplets. We will get them during phase two. The execution of the rich. Get me the men. I will take care of the cops. And Apollo. Now.'

'What?' Aristoteli asked.

'You heard me. You two were seen by the triplets. Go back to your cage. The police will find you just like all the other personnel. I will get off the island with our ship on the other side. I will see you both soon. The meeting is on the 12th of next month.'

Platonas wanted to get up and hug his father farewell. But, he knew his father wasn't the sentimental type. He saw him cry at his mother's funeral and that was the last tear he'd ever shed. For all Platonas knew, it might have well been his first. His father meant the world to him. The only family he had ever known. A lonely boy, home-schooled and with a passion for justice, all Platonas ever wished for, was to make his father proud.

Platonas ducked above his controls and pulled his mic closer. 'All army men, please report to base. I repeat, please report to base. Firearms, a must,' he announced and switched off his mic. By the time he swung his desk chair around, his father had walked out the door.

'Come on, junior. Let's get back to our cage. We'll have to make it seem like we were locked up just like everybody else working here,' Aristoteli said, patting him on the shoulder.

Chapter 30

'Pheew, we made it,' Apollo said with a wide smile as he gazed back; Hotel Murder, small and less menacing, was perched on the beach, far in the distance. 'No one seems to have followed us,' he added as he turned around, checking out the minor cave they stood in. Valentina sat upon an oddly shaped rock, mostly balancing on her feet. She placed her hands upon her knees and lowered her head, trying to catch her elusive breath.

Alexandro also looked back along their long route from the beach to the hills. Just hunting lizards and sand in the wind moved around. He grabbed Apollo by the neck and pushed him against the cave's wall. Dirt crumbled and fell upon Apollo's shoulders. Apollo coughed, lost in the sandy cloud. 'What the...?'

'Alexandro!' Valentina said, standing up.

'Spread out your arms or I will break them,' Alexandro ordered. 'Shut it,' he yelled as Apollo opened his mouth. 'The only words I want to hear from your mouth is the truth, or help me God, I will break you.'

Alexandro's muscles stretched, and his veins appeared along his arm. His fingers squeezed against the trembling throat he held tightly, and color began to leave Apollo. Valentina took a step sideways to look at Alexandro's face. She trusted him with her life.

He saved her in more ways than could be described. She never doubted him and remained silent.

'What's your role in all of this?'

'My... My role? I don't...'

Apollo did not manage to finish his reply as fingers closing in choked any words coming out.

'The truth.'

Apollo shook his head. 'What is it you think I can tell you?'

Alexandro let go of him and punched him hard in the stomach. Apollo fell to his knees. Alexandro kicked him in the face; blood and saliva sprayed the muddy wall behind them.

'I am not known for my patience. One more body will mean nothing after the two days we have had. Don't play with me.'

Apollo crawled and sat with his back against the wall. 'Okay, okay,' he said with his hands begging Alexandro to back off. 'I'm guessing the police told you who I am, then.'

Alexandro nodded and took a step forward.

'So, the police know,' he said louder, fixing his shirt's collar, checking that his transmitter was still in place. *All I have to do is stall them, until my men arrive,* he thought.

'Unbelievable. You piece of shit. You knew?' Valentina said, resisting acting out like her hot-tempered boyfriend.

Apollo wore his sorrowful expression on his face and opened his watery puppy eyes, looking at her. 'No excuses, Valentina. Yes, I am a part of all this. This is my revenge.'

'Revenge for what? What twisted mind does something like this? And, why the hell are we here with you? Planning on murdering us out here? We weren't on your broadcasting schedule, so we get slaughtered like animals in a cave?' Turning to Alexandro, she added, 'Babe, check this bastard for weapons.'

Apollo stretched out his arms. 'No, no, it's not like that. I was never going to kill you. You are innocent. Hardworking folk. My plan was to get you out and hide with you until we were rescued.'

'Make you a believable survivor, right? You arranged it so you were left with the cops?' Alexandro asked, frisking him for any hidden guns.

'Something like that,' he replied.

'That's why Maximos and Theodore were taken while we slept?' Valentina asked.

Apollo nodded in return.

'You spoke of revenge. What the hell happens to someone to justify so many murders? Gruesome killings...'

Apollo blew out air from behind closed teeth. 'My name is Simos Lemoni. Husband of Despoina Lemoni.' He paused, looking for a reaction in their eyes. Both were taken back and exchanged a sorrowful look between them. They knew the story. At least how the media presented and sold the urban tragedy. 'Debts were crashing down on us. We were both unlawfully fired without any sign of compensation. We struggled to feed our kids. My two beautiful baby girls...' he said, the last words fighting to escape his lips. Real tears fell from his eyes and died in his short beard. He looked away and continued. 'When we lost our house to the bank, food was so scarce, we feared for our children. Foolish of me, I guess, but as jobs were hard to find, especially during the first years of the crisis, I decided to rob a supermarket. I did not take cash, just food, and supplies for the baby. Two years! Two years, I got. A family man with two kids to feed. And, you know what the judge told me? The system will take care of your family. Yeah, the system bloody well did.'

He was panting. His fingers clenched into tight fists. His nails digging into his skin.

Valentina sat down back upon her rock. 'What did you tell her that day? The police said you called her that evening from prison. Was it one of your sick games? Did you...?'

'How dare you? My Lina was three, and my Antonia was an infant. You fucking better...' Apollo yelled and stood up. Alexandro pushed him back. 'Watch it,' he warned him.

'You truly believe I would want my own wife to murder my angels? Not a day goes by without me dreaming of them. Seeing them in a park or on a beach, playing carelessly and laughing with their stomachs full. And now, they rot in their tiny coffins. I will never see them smile again, go to school, marry...'

Apollo let out a scream and turned and hit the wall. 'You really want to know what I said that day? I called her for support. I was raped that day. I was sent to Korydallo Prison with all the murderers and rapists. All I did wrong was step on a guy's foot by mistake in the prison cafeteria. I still remember his sinister smile when he said he would see me later. I was alone in the shower when this gang leader had his men beat me up. Four men lifted me up and threw me upon the locker room table. They bent me over and watched as their leader viciously raped me. And, you think that was punishment enough? They all had their way with me. I was fucked to near death for stepping on a guy's shoe,' Apollo said, wiping his eyes. 'Want to feel disgust? He came on his boot and forced me to lick it off. Lick my boots clean he said, and they all laughed.'

Apollo closed his eyes, unable to talk anymore. Alexandro turned to check the horizon. All clear as far as his eyes could see. He approached Valentina and put his arm around her waist. He knew well she was distraught.

'And you told her this?'

Apollo turned around, removing his fingers from the dirt wall. 'Not in such detail. She was my everything, you see,' he said, looking at them with a warm gaze. 'We were like you. Madly in love. She was my best friend. I was fucking bleeding out my ass, and I needed to hear her voice. To give me strength. And all I did was take hers away. It was the final blow. She felt life was over. That things would never improve. The world became a hostile, dangerous, scary place and she did not want her girls to live in it anymore. She was a firm believer that heaven was a real place. All she was doing was sending our girls there, saving them from all this.'

'I feel for you. I truly do,' Valentina said. 'But for me, there is no excuse for murder. You slaughtered all those people. Or at least you had a role in their deaths.'

'Not anyone innocent. They...'

'We heard your bullshit accusations in the broadcast. Save your breath, man. You are going back to prison. And this time, it will be for life. And, you know what?' Alexandro asked and walked up to Apollo. 'I hope your gang leader is there waiting for you.'

With that said, he grabbed Apollo again by the neck. 'Now, I will be calling the police and informing them of everything. How many armed men are in the hotel? Speak!' he shouted.

Apollo did not reply. He just smiled and chuckled. The next sound that echoed in the cave was the cocking of a gun. Alexandro turned and saw three armed men standing by the cave's entrance. He let Apollo go, took a step sideways and stood in front of Valentina.

Chapter 31

Hours ago...

Sometimes the words we leave unspoken are the ones that should have been said.

I saw this saying every moment on Tracy's coffee mug. I have never been a fan of motivational quotes, but after everything said and done, those fourteen words floated around my mind.

After leaving SERENITY nursing home, Ioli and I finally spoke. I informed her about my visit to Simos Lemoni's mother. I told her why the house was familiar to her.

'It was the house where Despoina Lemoni murdered her children. Her husband Simos was in prison at the time. He was released just three weeks before our billionaire received the message from the house.'

'Yes, but was it him? Did he return to his home? There's no way to prove...'

'His mother seems to think he is dangerous. She kept on going on about how her Apollo wanted revenge against the system. Something about killing the rich. She hasn't seen him since then. I'm telling you this is our guy.'

Ioli stopped in the middle of the street; loud honks bringing her out of shock. She rushed across the street and sat down on a green wooden bench. 'Apollo? I thought his name was Simos?'

'Yeah, Apollo was his nickname. His mother called him that ever since a child. Handsome and muscular and all that. Why do you ask?'

'Remember at the meeting when you left the conference room, and I was talking about the surveillance video? The guy named Apollo by the voice, never appears on camera. Just once do we see his feet. We see people talking to him, but never his face. Boss, it's not a popular name, and now you say this Apollo talked about revenge on the rich? This could be our other guy, too.'

It was a leap, yet not a big one.

Logic would say that a poor, released inmate would need money to set up a scheme like Hotel Murder. Maybe that is how our billionaire came into the picture.

We met back at headquarters, both rushing into Captain Savva's office to explain our theory.

Soon, all tech personnel were searching through our billionaire's property listings. Three privately owned islands appeared.

'Can we trace which one is not covered by a national phone signal?' Ioli asked.

'All three are covered. However, they could be using some kind of blocking device. Something like that can be traced. It will show up on certain wave transmissions. Give us time to check,' a woman with thick red glasses replied, her eyes never leaving her computer's screen.

'Kato Antikeri,' she said finally.

Just the sound of the island brought relief to the team. Days hoping, searching, wishing for where Hotel Murder was and now it was uttered, released to us.

Orders for multiple task forces were given and a rescue mission was planned.

'Can we get the signal back up?' Ioli asked.

'We could get the Hellenic Telecommunication Organization to boost their signal, depending on where their transmitters are.'

'Great. You do that. Then I can call and warn Alexandro.'

Chapter 32

'How cute,' the tall guy in the middle said. 'Everybody out, now,' he ordered with a croaky voice.

Alexandro took Valentina by the hand and cautiously exited into the brightening sunlight. Apollo followed, complaining to the men that they took too long.

'Shut up, Simos,' the tall, fifty year old said. 'The police are on their way.'

'I know. So kill these idiots and let's be going.'

'Yes, all loose ends must be disposed of,' the big guy said and turned his firearm, pointing it in Apollo's face.

'What the fuck do you think you're doing? Guys, remove his weapon,' Apollo ordered the two men. Both men did not move. Both remained still with their guns pointed at Valentina and Alexandro. Valentina watched as the sunrays danced upon the shiny, new pistols. She placed her head upon Alexandro's broad back and gazed out to the endless sea. She wanted her last feeling, her last smell, her last view to be a pleasant one.

'I am your boss, I am the motherfucker that is paying you!' Apollo yelled, waving his arms. 'What the hell is wrong with you guys? This is my plan, our plan!'

'The plan is so much bigger than you, them or me, Simos. Larger than all of us. Society has been shocked. Nothing can go wrong. Even if a single camera caught a glimpse of you, we are screwed. With your past and connections to Despoina's story, you are worth more as a martyr. We need no hero. We need no leader. Let it go, Simos. Go join your girls,' the olive-skinned man with the big mole below his right ear said.

A loud bang scattered through the valley of sand and bushes. Apollo's head cracked open before their eyes, and parts of his brain and skin fell to the ground; a meal for nature's creatures later that day. His body remained upright for a second, and then gravity pulled Apollo's lifeless body to the ground. A pool of blood came and colored the sandy ground.

'Who are you?' Alexandro asked, hoping to buy time.

The tall man chuckled. 'It doesn't really matter, you see, my young boy. Who I am, who they are. We are Greece United. We are what every Greek's dream should be. We are an idea. A utopia to come,' he said proudly. 'And, I am sorry, my sweetheart, but you cannot be a part of it,' he continued, tilting his head and looking at Valentina. 'Bring them here,' he said to his men. 'The police know about Apollo being Simos Lemoni, so let's make this look like a showdown between him and the cops.'

His men waved their guns and ordered them to move.

'Stand exactly there,' the tall man said, his calm voice annoying Alexandro.

'Face Simos, Apollo, whatever. Perfect,' he said and turned to his men. 'You will stand here, where Simos was. Now, shoot them. Heart or brain, please.'

Chapter 33

Meanwhile, back at the mansion, I stood behind the young officers burning through the front door of Hotel Murder.

'Come on, quickly,' I said, my hands tightly around my pistol. Four officers stood behind me, also ready to fire.

The Special Forces team had spread out around the mansion.

With a soft clang, a piece of the protective metal shutter fell to the fake-grass carpet outside the main entrance.

'Enter with caution,' I said and ducked into the newly-opened doorway; a reddish, melted-steel arch leading into the murderous surrounding.

'Clear,' Pauline said, switching on the lights, her rifle extended down the corridor.

One by one, we broke down locked doors and searched the rooms.

Most were empty.

Most.

The ones that were not still haunt my hardened soul.

A stench of death enveloped us as we were faced with mutilated bodies. Human beings tortured and executed without hesitation. Like bringing down your thumb on an ant running along your kitchen counter.

Down in the basement, the Special Forces team found twelve members of personnel caged behind bars. They had been locked in, in groups of two or three, separated and left without food, water or light for two days. Left in desperation, they were highly dehydrated and exhausted from screaming and crying. They were escorted out of the dungeons of hell and brought outside to the timid, winter sun, to refreshing water, to the experienced police medics. Smiles of relief and tears of joy painted their exit. Most had given up hope of surviving. In the darkness, they sat and heard each execution, knowing that their chances of being let go were minimal. Regret is a small word to describe how they felt about accepting their position.

'As soon as possible, we need testimonies. As soon as the medics give you the okay, get their stories,' I said to the officers beside me and with Pauline following me, I headed to the last locked door of the long corridor.

Inside, Clio opened her eyes wide, warning her brother to cease complaining that no one was coming. Her plan had to work. *It just has to,* she thought, mentally unable to think of a scenario where her brothers would be killed in front of her eyes. A scenario where her frail-hearted father would watch her be executed on live television.

Pauline, a woman a foot taller than me and with broader shoulders, kicked down the door and I rushed into the room, my gun extended. A young girl lay in the middle of the room.

No blood, could she be alive?

Suddenly, I felt movement behind me. I figured it was Pauline entering after me.

Then, I heard her shout. 'Freeze!'

I turned to see one of the Afroudaki boys ready to jump me. He froze on the spot. Another young man was by the door and made a move on Pauline.

'Don't!' I yelled, hoping that Pauline's perfect reflexes did not kick in. After all this, to get shot by the police. Pauline's finger stopped a hair away from the trigger. 'Athens Police,' I said and showed the triplets my badge.

Clio sat up straight and started to cry. She leaped off the ground and ran into my arms. I embraced the trembling girl as her brothers began to laugh out hysterically. Pauline took a step back, making sure neither ran into her muscular arms.

On the floor above, officers nodded to each other and approached an old, wooden closet. Mumbling could be heard from inside. Silently, they took slow steps towards it. The female voice grew louder.

'...our daily bread. Forgive us our sins, as we forgive those who sin against us. Lead us not into temptation, but deliver us from evil.'

A short officer pulled back the door. Salome shrieked in fear and covered her face with her hands.

'Ma'am, we are with the metropolitan police. We are here to rescue you.'

Salome looked up at the figure towering over her, the light from the bulb above forming a halo around his head.

'My savior,' she said and reached out.

The man lifted her up as Salome praised the Lord for her salvage from the depths of hell into which she had sunk.

Below, the three siblings held hands as they exited the hotel. A deafening, juddering sound swooped from above. The police helicopter had arrived to make its rounds over the island. I looked up and saw Ioli, sitting by the chopper's open door. She waved, and I forced a smile. Alexandro and Valentina were no-where to be found. SWAT team members entered the secret passage and reached the end. They exited and looked around. No one was to be seen. I could see Ioli's eyes searching in the crowd below. The helicopter flew above the hotel and vanished from my sight.

Where are they?

*****

Panayioti Karaoli had killed many times before. Never a human, though. A hunting fan, with thirty-five years of hunting and trapping under his belt, he was an excellent shot. Now, he stood with a gun in his hands just meters away from his prey. Two humans. Two cops. And, he was ordered to shoot them. Heart or brains, the boss said. He gently blew out air and mentally prepared for the deadly shots. His mind travelled back to his village, to his four underage kids and his unemployed wife. He did not care for the cause. He was there for the large paycheck. *A week's work, a year's salary. Shoot them and get it over with, Panayioti,* his inner voice prepared him.

As his finger squeezed down on the trigger, his arm shook by the rattling of the helicopter approaching. 'Police, drop your weapons!' the order came from the speakers above.

The first bullet escaped his gun and hit Alexandro in the chest. The bullet's kick pushed him back, and he tripped over Valentina's leg. Alexandro fell to the ground. Valentina screamed as Ioli and the men in the chopper opened fire on the three men.

As Panayioti took a bullet to the head and his body violently shook and fell, his partner shot back at the helicopter, while his boss shot at Valentina putting pressure on Alexandro's open wound. *No witnesses*, he thought as he shot her and dived into the cave, hoping to escape through the dark tunnels that led out to sea. He would not be that lucky. Ioli's bullet followed him as he stepped into the cave, hitting him in his neck. His last breath departed from his lips as his mind thought of Platonas. He died, sure that his son would continue his mission.

'Get us down there, now,' Ioli yelled to the pilot. 'Call for medics,' she continued yelling at the officer by her side.

Valentina's back welcomed the penetrating bullet, and with a silent gasp, she fell upon Alexandro.

Ioli looked from above as the helicopter descended to the sandy ground. In all the chaos and racket, she watched the dying couple as if someone had pressed the mute button.

Valentina had let go of his wound and blood oozed out quickly. Alexandro coughed out blood, and his chest moved violently up and down as his blood-filled lungs fought for oxygen. His hand dug into his pocket and with his remaining strength, he pulled out the jewelry box that he had hidden in his pocket since their arrival on the island. His quivering thumb pushed the ring box lid open. He lifted the red velvet box for Valentina to see. Valentina placed her head upon his bloody chest, feeling his weak heartbeat. A smile ran along her pale face. 'Yes, yes. A million times yes,' she said and struggled to raise her head. 'Yes, yes,' she raised her voice, making sure that he could hear her. She dragged her body higher up upon his and looked down into the eyes she loved getting lost in. Alexandro was unable to speak, but his smile and the shine in his eyes revealed that he had heard her. Valentina closed her eyes and lay a kiss upon his lips. As she opened her eyes, she saw the dead expression clouding his youthful face. She stroked his cheek, her finger playing with his deep dimples, the ones she found irresistible when her stare first fell upon the muscular, short, 'I take no shit' cop from the mainland. 'Goodbye, my love,' she said and closed her eyes, giving up hope, letting the pain in her back take over.

Ioli ran towards them screaming their names. With shaking hands, she checked for a pulse. Alexandro, her rookie partner, the young officer she had trained, dead. She then pushed back Valentina's blonde hair and placed her bloody fingers upon her neck.

And there it was.

Frail, weak, an undertone.

'Medics, quick. She is still alive...'

Chapter 34

The following day – Ending 1

I woke up feeling like most Greeks that rainy, foggy morning. Numb. Mentally numb.

Like waking up from a vivid, lucid nightmare and trying to convince yourself nothing of it was true.

Yet, it all was.

A terrorist organization had unleashed its evil upon Greece. People were executed on live TV. Every day people voted for them to die. It was seven in the morning, and the countless discussions had not ceased from the previous day. The morning news was the last thing I needed to witness. We had lost one of our own. Alexandro was dead, and Valentina's life was held by the thread of life support. She could not breathe on her own. Fortunately, if I may use such a word in such a situation, doctors were optimistic. My wife, Tracy, twitched as I disrupted her sleeping position. Yet, she did not wake. Her subtle snoring resumed, and I crept out of the dark bedroom.

In my navy blue boxers, I walked barefooted into the kitchen, leaving the warmth of the carpet and stepping on the cold, tiled floor. With eyes half shut –or half open, if you're one of those optimist types- I brewed myself a nice, hot, strong Greek coffee and indulged in breathing in its rich aroma. I stuffed down a couple of

Digestive Whole Grain biscuits, called my session a breakfast and was ready to return to the bedroom to deliver Tracy's coffee and get dressed for work when my phone began to vibrate.

Unknown caller, but familiar numbering. One of the many extensions from police headquarters.

'Captain Papacosta,' I said, trying to sound more awake than I really was.

'Morning, sir. Sorry for the early call. It's Helen from the front desk. We just received a phone call from the hospital, and to be honest, I wasn't sure who to inform. Her family is arriving mid-day from what I know, and I did not wish to wake the chief...'

She was mumbling. She was killing bees without going for the honey. 'What happened?'

I sat down and bowed my head. I rubbed my forehead and squeezed between my eyes. 'Thank you for calling me,' I said as she reached the end of her sentence.

I wished I had it in me to curse.

I wished I still smoked.

Ten minutes later, I set off for Ioli's house. I switched off the car stereo and let the downpour and my wipes provide the music. I parked outside her place and called her, informing her that I was outside. I knew she would be awake. An early bird, even before having a child, she answered after only one beep.

'What are you doing outside?' she said, closed the phone and appeared at the door. She signalled to me to be quiet as I walked in the rain towards her. 'He just drank his milk. If left alone, he goes back to sleep,' she said.

'Mark?' I asked about her husband.

'At the hospital. Ten-hour shift from last night. He should be home, soon. Then our thirty minutes of meeting up and I will be off to work.'

I nodded and sat down on her orange living room sofa.

'What brings you here so early in the morning?' she asked, and her eyes tried to read me. 'What's wrong?' her second question came as she sat down by me.

'I got a call this morning from HQ. The hospital called. Valentina woke up last night...'

'Sweet Jesus, that's great...' she began to say, then saw my face. 'Complications?'

I shook my head. 'No, no. Er.. Okay, there's no easy way. She woke last night and as soon as the doctors left her to relax and get some sleep, she switched off her oxygen machine and her monitor. Doctors figure she died calmly in her sleep half an hour later...'

'Why? Fuck, why?' Ioli said, standing up.

'Apparently, she left a voice message on her phone addressed to her parents, apologizing, but she did not wish to live a life that did not include Alexandro.'

Ioli chuckled. 'She hated that small island of hers, she did. Wow, true love, huh?'

'True love,' I replied.

Ioli walked over to the kitchen door. 'Whiskey and ice?' she asked.

I opened my mouth to speak and she shot me down.

'Don't say anything about the time. Alcohol goes by occasion and circumstance, not a number on a ticking clock!'

Two days later – Ending 2

'The suspect is on foot and entering an old, abandoned warehouse down at the old docks. He seems cautious, on edge. He parked miles away. More people seem to be inside...'

Police officer Taso Anastasiou spoke into his walkie-talkie. Together with his partner, they were one of the three teams following Platonas Pappas. We had not released any details, at least any formal details of what happened on the island. We wanted Platonas to believe that his father had made it off the island. It wasn't hard to identify the bodies and discover his next of kin. The Afroudaki triplets and Salome all paused on Platonas's photo and confirmed that he was the man that took them to Hotel Murder.

'This is team B,' another voice came through the speaker at Headquarters. 'We can confirm Aristoteli Minoa is also in the building.'

We needed no more.

Special Forces surrounded the building within twenty minutes. Soon, old rusty doors were smashed in, and gunshots were exchanged.

Aristoteli took a stray bullet to the throat. A fitting end to his voice. Platonas survived with bullet wounds decorating the back of his legs. A ricocheting bullet doing most of the damage. He ended up losing both. A legless inmate for life.

The entire leadership of Greece United dead or arrested. Men and women with a sinister common goal.

Greece accepted another shock. Among those arrested, the prime minister's daughter, two police captains and an army general stood out. Greece United was just about to get started. Hotel Murder was going to be just the beginning. The terrorist group kept records of their every move, past and future.

And with the end of the terrorist case came closure to our billionaire case. It was Apollo who murdered our missing billionaire. It was his funds and his island that made everything possible. To recruit experts in electronics, army missionaries, to set up Hotel Murder. Apollo forced the old man to secretly transfer hidden Swiss money to accounts used by Greece United.

We could only pray that it was truly an end to the murderous group.

Two weeks later – The final end

Athens wore its Christmas coat well.

As if ticking off a magical check-list. Chilly wind with fragile, short-lived snowflakes? Check. Rays of sun escaping from behind roaming clouds, illuminating the horizon of snowy mountains? Check. Giant Christmas tree dead center of Syntagma square? Check. Christmas lights all along Ermou, the city's busiest shopping street? Check. Carol singers? Check. Smiling –even faking it for their kids- people? Check.

Yes, Christmas suited the grey, dull city well.

This year, Christmas also brought Greece back to its normal, daily rhythms. Greece United took a hard blow on society, and though the dents were still there, wounds had begun to heal. Life always goes on.

Ioli had called me and asked to meet up for a coffee. Which in Ioli's case –and much to my delight- meant coffee, then cake, a long walk, then kebabs and ice-cold Mythos beers.

You could say, I am a man that takes risks. However, I am no fool. I wasn't crazy enough to drive into the town center and lose my day stuck in traffic. I walked in the light drizzle, enjoying the icy droplets splaying on my thin hair and running along my face, getting caught up in my new-found wrinkles. Shallow, worm-like cavities, near invisible from a foot away, but still wrinkles. I knew they were there. They 'good morning' me in the mirror ever since I hit the big 5-0. Age or chemotherapy? Both? Who knew? They had been multiplying ever since. I walked to the nearest Metro station, and down into the ground I descended. Soon, I came back up to the surface at Monastiraki station. The stone-built church welcomed me to its square, with its thousand shoppers rushing to finish their shopping lists. Beggars ambled among them, their tin cup extended up front. The row of homeless near the church had vanished. Local police had removed them from all shopping and tourist areas. Athens knew well to hide its true colors from the foreigners visiting the grand city.

I was just in time to witness the last small snowflakes floating around in the air. Soon, the light drizzle from my house had followed me into town and picked up strength along the way. I headed for Plaka, and Yiasemi cafe. With the Acropolis standing majestically above me, I entered the coffee shop. The warmth from inside hugged me as I entered. The fireplace was hosting a generous log fire. Ioli was already there. She raised her hand and waved, her woolly hat still on her head. She had also just arrived.

'Hey,' I said, sitting down.

'Hey, yourself. Find parking? Took me forever and I finally decided to betray my principles.'

'No!' I acted as if in shock. 'You paid for parking?'

She nodded, and I chuckled. 'What did you expect? Christmas. I took the Metro.'

'Clever you,' she replied, taking off her brown coat and placing it on the back of her chair. 'To be honest, I wasn't expecting such... hmm... prosperity.'

'I know what you mean, but don't forget, even if twenty percent can't afford to have Christmas this year, in a city of four million that's eight hundred thousand people.'

Ioli whistled upon hearing the number. 'But, consider this,' I continued. 'There's three point two million that can. And, even if only that rich ten percent is out on the streets shopping, that's four hundred thousand, plus the tourists and visitors from other towns...'

'Arghhh, no more statistics, please. I get your point, Show mercy,' she joked.

Just then we became aware of the brawny waiter standing by our table, waiting for us to notice him. Ioli ordered our coffees and two pieces of baklava, while I gazed around at the fairy-light-decked interior with the jasmine vines and the shiny white lights. The blend of aromas invaded my nose. Jasmine flowers, burning wood and steamy coffees. A war of scents.

'So, what's up? I asked as the waiter left our round table for two.

'During coffee,' she said and smiled enigmatically.

'Okay, Mona Lisa. I have something to discuss also. I've been meaning to tell you but never had the guts. But, you're right. Let's wait for coffee.'

Ioli sat up straight, placed her arms on the cherry-wood table and leaned slightly forward. 'You love scaring me, huh? Just tell me now, that it's not your cancer again.'

'It's not cancer.'

Thankfully for Ioli's nerves, coffees and sweets arrived soon. We took our first sips in silence and then Ioli placed her porcelain cup back on its diamond-shaped plate.

'I'm tired...'

'Logical. You're a working mother, married to a doctor who spends more hours at the hospital than at home...'

'I'm tired of dead bodies,' she interrupted me. 'The game doesn't excite me anymore. Solving the mystery and getting the bad guy. I feel like I've played my part. I gave my all to serve and protect.' She paused. I said nothing. The load on her chest hadn't departed yet. She took another sip. 'I've asked to be transferred. No more homicides, for me. I wish for a desk job. With normal office hours...'

I opened my mouth, ready to speak. 'Wait!' she said.

'Before you judge me and try to change my mind by saying how good I am at it or say some perfect, guru-style line of support and make me love and appreciate you more, hear me out. I'm pregnant...'

My eyes lit up. 'Really? That's great...'

'Only two weeks late, no one knows yet. But, you see, I was already thinking of taking a break from murders. Then, Alexandro died before my eyes, and I thought, for sure, a break is needed. Then, this,' she said, placing her right hand on her belly. 'And, I started thinking, a desk job isn't all that bad. I will work while the kids are at school and get to be with them in the evening.'

I placed my hand upon hers. 'You know you are more than a partner to me. You're my friend, the adult daughter I never had.'

Tears gathered in her bright eyes. 'That's why it's so hard to quit homicide. It feels like I am quitting you. Deserting you.'

'I'm retiring early.'

'What?' she yelled, and heads around us turned. I smiled and took a chunk out of my delicious, honey-dripping slice of baklava. 'What do you mean?' she asked again, lowering her decibels.

'I'm there with you. Same stage. Lord knows I have had more than my fair share of death. I've lost a child, I've beaten cancer, I've broken up and gotten back with my wife. Now, I just want to garden, cook and read books. Enjoy time with Tracy, go away on holidays with her. Visit Greek islands and investigate beaches and restaurants, not murder suspects. And the timing is good. The new compensation plan isn't half bad, and after my father's death, my mother sold our family home back in New York and moved in with my sister. She divided the money between me and my sisters. Besides, I don't spend much and it's just Tracy and I.'

Ioli sat back and exhaled deeply.

'Haven't you got anything to say?' I asked the strong, opinionated Cretan woman before me.

'I think, we should have skipped coffee and went straight to beers,' she said and we both laughed. A laughter from lighter chests. 'So, this is officially the end of our Greek island mysteries adventure?'

I nodded. 'Sounds so.' Then, I chuckled. 'Greek island mysteries? You're a weird one, Cara.'

'Always rich coming from you, boss.'

I took another sip and smiled.

'What you grinning about?' she asked, finally biting into her dessert.

'Actually, that title is growing on me. Maybe, in between cooking and gardening, I could pick up writing. The Greek Island Mysteries...'

Ioli looked up and laughed. 'You better make me sound sexy and smart, or I will be suing your ass for royalties.'

THE END

March

of Revenge

(A short story from Greek Island Mysteries #6 – Available now)

Protaras, Cyprus

March, 2018

Murder in paradise is as hideous as everywhere else.

Fig Tree Bay's warm hug embraced few swimmers this time of year; its high season beginning in a month or so. The island's best waters lingered in the small bay. Clear, pure, caressing the golden sand beach and carrying the freshness of the Mediterranean Sea.

The Bay's prominent fig trees glowed as they welcomed the rising sun's first rays of the day. Few workers had parked on the hill towering the bay and were busy opening up their restaurants, souvenir shops and ice-cream parlors.

A rental car parked between them; its red number plates separating it from the others. Tourists.

'I can't believe you woke us up so early,' the teenage girl whined, rubbing her eyes below her dark shades.

'We don't even wake up this early on school days,' her younger brother added.

'Well, if we were back in England, that's exactly where you would be going in an hour,' his mother said, stepping out of the vehicle. 'Remember, this is all about your father celebrating his promotion. We promised to go along with whatever he wished,' she continued, massaging her husband's bare back as he stood in front of her enjoying the view offered by Greek Mother Nature.

'What a glorious sunrise! Come on. A quick, cool morning swim and then... breakfast. Mmm, I can smell the bacon and hash browns already.'

The girl rolled her eyes. 'The shops haven't even opened yet!'

Her father ignored her remark and began to jog down the covered-in-beach-sand, wooden-plaque path.

His wife remained smiling as she followed him and settled their beach bag, their *borrowed* hotel towels and her straw hat on two sunbeds, just meters from the tranquil sea. Her smile vanished as she dipped her toes into the pool-like waters.

'Jesus Christ, it's freezing!'

Both her children laughed as they rushed by her and dove in. Their father joined them and soon, the gang of three splashed away; attacking their matriarch as she ambled past them, acting brave, accepting their usual attack of cold water.

With a deep exhale, she plunged out of their sight and resurfaced away from them.

'Anyone up for swimming to the island?' she asked, pointing to the uninhabited islet that dominated the waters of the cove.

'Too early for exercising,' her daughter replied and swam out back to shore to add more sunscreen to her pale skin.

Her son shook his head. 'I'm hungry.'

'The restaurant hasn't opened yet,' his father replied. 'Want to build a sand castle?'

His son nodded with a smile and rushed out of the sea to fetch his beach toys.

'See you later, dear,' his wife said and began swimming away, soon to be standing on the first rock, covered with low vegetation. The squawking of the colony of seagulls caught her attention. Her blue, beady eyes squinted as she tried to focus among their thin legs and long beaks.

'Is that a seal? What are they eating?' she asked aloud as the breeze carried over a stench that reminded her of the miasma that had hung around her run-over cat.

She hopped from rock to rock until her wet feet landed upon the plectrum-shaped island. She turned to see her family. All three covered in sand, building away their Neverland. Other swimmers had made their appearance, too, while the restaurant had finally opened. Her tummy was rumbling, yet she would never admit such a thing as it would set off her kids.

'One look and I'm heading back.'

Steady step after steady step, she approached the birds. Her presence scaring enough of them as to reveal their feast.

Quiet Susan –as her family and friends often referred to her by, never knew she could scream that loud. She fell back and sat in shock as she covered her eyes. That is where her husband found her and wrapped his strong arms around her trembling body. Together they swam back to shore and asked the Cypriot waiter, standing at the restaurant's entrance, to notify the police.

*****

The lifeguard boat danced upon the waves of the open waters by the islet. Chief Inspector Demetriou stood on the bow of the twelve-meter boar, ready to disembark onto the rocky island. She watched as her partner, Sergeant Nick Nicolaou swam the short distance from shore, in full uniform. She shook her head, strikes of blond hair escaping her black sports cap, exhaled and whispered to the forensic officer behind them. 'Why do I get all the weirdos?'

'He says he is afraid of boats and gets seasick,' the young man in full white uniform explained. Demetriou bit her bottom lip, rolled her eyes, tucked away renegade hair and jumped off the boat. With arms wide open, she did her best to scare away the seagulls. The corpse lay naked. She approached the body, hoping the eyes were shut. She was new to homicide; only seven months in the department after years in internal affairs. Three bodies with open eyes so far and all three stalked her nightmares. As she placed the white rubber glove on her right hand, the young forensic officer's voice came from behind her.

'I thought they said it was a female body,' he commented, looking at the manly chest and hairy left leg before him.

'His genitals have been cut off,' Demetriou said. 'That and his long hair must have confused the tourist lady. She did say, she did not come that close.'

'I don't blame her,' he replied, squatting by the mutilated dead man with the multiple stab wounds.

Demetriou pulled the man's black hair from his face. 'Holy Mary, protect us,' she said and placed her right hand on her necklace's silver cross. 'His eyes have been removed, too!'

'The seagulls?'

'I doubt it. The sockets look stabbed. Look at the knife marks here...'

She paused, sensing a presence behind her. A shadow moved alongside and then covered her. She could hear the drops of sea water falling from her partner, landing on the dry rock, living just for seconds under the sizzling, merciless Cypriot sun.

'Isn't that Thomas Keravnos?' he said, breathless and soaking wet.

'Who?' they both asked.

'The Ayia Napa mafia drug lord,' he replied, squeezing the bottom of his white shirt, releasing a short-lived pour.

Demetriou gazed at the ashen, bird-bitten, eyeless face of the fifty-something man. 'You're right,' she said, feeling slightly guilty at the tones of joy coloring her voice. She was not the type to wish the death of anybody, but she did feel relief that this was not some poor family man and was probably the result of a drug deal dispute.

*****

News nowadays did not have to wait. Not for the evening news, nor the morning papers. Stories of interest spread like a digital wildfire; online flames jumping from device to device. Thomas Keravnos's death was such a story.

A notorious business man, he was a popular sports figure on the eastern Mediterranean island. For his fans, he was a former footballer who made a fortune in tourism and bought his beloved team, leading them many times to the league title. For his employees at his hotels, casino, bars and night clubs, he was a generous boss who offered hefty bonuses on top of above-average wages. However, for society, the media and the police, he was as dirty as they came. Human trafficking, illegal prostitution and drugs were known activities of his. Yet none ever proven in court.

Prestigious lawyer Adonis Stylianou already felt tired that morning. With only two clients down and twelve to go, he locked his office door, stepped out onto the little side balcony on the 17th floor of Ayia Napa's Marina West Tower and lit a much-needed second cigarette of the day. His right hand snuck in his robe's pocket and he lifted out his iPhone. 'Let me check my bets,' he whispered aloud. As he activated his Wi-Fi signal, multiple notifications flashed across the top of the screen. 'Death of gangster?' he read the title that caught his attention. As the link opened, his knees felt weak. He stumbled back a step or two and sat down upon the air conditioning unit that occupied a third of the small balcony. His eyes watered up. He exhaled deeply. 'Got what you deserved, you fat bastard!'

He lit another cigarette with the dying end of his previous one, ignoring his office telephone. His mind could not be further from his socialite client's divorce papers. He looked down at his wedding ring. A year as a widow had gone by and it still decorated his index finger. Love, guilt or both, he could not find the courage to slide it off. Unable to move on, once again, his mind drifted to *that* night.

Protaras, Cyprus
March, 2017

Adonis paced up and down his hotel room. His wife, Kate, was still getting ready. His green eyes fixed on his black Rolex. Cold sweat was forming on his wide forehead and conquering his armpits. The room was cool; his heart was not.

'*What the hell are you doing, Adonis?*'

His wild thoughts were driving him crazy. His hands, unable to remain still. He headed over to the mini bar. 'Famous Grouse and Jack Daniels. Great,' he whispered and opened both miniature bottles, devouring their contents in seconds.

He wiped away his tears and headed to the bedroom's door. Kate looked stunning in her red dress. Her short, brown hair caressed her bare shoulders as she placed on her gold earrings.

'I have no idea,' she said, leaning closer to her cell phone.

'Well, whatever Adonis has planned for you tonight, have a good time,' her sister replied and with the sound of kisses, Kate ended the call.

Adonis could not bear to step into the room. *'Maybe I should call it all off? She's my wife!'*

Kate swung the leather chair round with her legs and stared at her nervous-looking husband. 'Okay, what's the matter with you? You've been acting weird all week. At first, I thought, oh no, he's lost more money on gambling, then you told me that you booked a remote motel for us to have a quiet weekend getaway and I thought, okay, all is good. Now, we are here and you haven't said a word to me all day. I don't even know where we are going tonight.'

Adonis swallowed the lump forming in his throat; his Adam apple bouncing like a yo-yo as he searched for words. Outside, a car could be heard driving into the empty car park. Headlights danced upon the motel's thin curtains and light fell on Adonis's guilty face.

'We're not going anyway,' he managed to say with a weak voice. Kate squinted her eyes and tilted her head slightly to her right. 'I did lose money. A lot,' he continued, raising his voice. The slamming of car doors outside adding haste to his words. 'I won a few rounds and got cocky,' he added louder, interrupting his wife as she stood and started to complain about his addiction. 'I went into the high-ballers room. I kept on winning and ended up on the main table in the back... with Thomas Keravnos.'

Kate sat back down and placed her ashen face in her cold hands. Thomas Keravnos. Her ex-boss. 'How much did you lose?'

'The house, the office...'

'What?' she yelled, looking out.

'But, I made a deal. A last bet. He gave me a chance....'

Kate stood up. 'Go on, what chance?'

Footsteps could be heard outside their door. Adonis exhaled, closed his eyes and unleashed his heart. 'A night with you.'

Kate stood motionless for a second or two. A smile was born upon her coral, red lips. A smile that grew into a giggle and then laughter. 'You're joking, right? Pulling my leg? Is this one of your sick jokes that I am supposed to find funny?'

The knocking on the old wooden door came as her answer.

Kate's eyes opened wide. 'You're mad! I'm your wife, you dumb, weak cunt!'

'He always fancied you. Had a thing for you from back in the day when you worked for him. It's just sex. Ten minutes and we save our house and our savings...'

'Then you sleep with him! I'm out of here,' she said and walked past him, spitting at his feet. 'I'm done. We're done. I'm going to my mother's and on Monday, I'm divorcing you!'

Another thud was heard from the door. The sound of keys followed and the motel door was pushed open.

Kate stood in the middle of the room. Three men entered the room. Thomas and two hefty bodyguards.

'Close the door,' he ordered in his distinct, croaky voice.

'*He owns the place*,' Kate thought, looking as his bodyguard used the motel's master key to lock the door. 'Mister Thomas, there has been a misunderstanding. My fool of a husband, does not own me. I am not up for this. I'm sorry he wasted your time. Take our house, take his money, take him and break his legs. I don't care, but I am not sleeping with you...'

'I won you fair and square.'

Kate bit her bottom lip and stepped back as he approached her. 'This is illegal. You can't win a person. If you touch me, I'll scream.'

Thomas smiled and his eyes glowed. All he said was 'boys', and both men came at her. They picked her up by her arms and forced her into the bedroom. Kate shrieked, kicked and even managed to bite one of the men. He replied with a strong punch to her face. She fell back onto the cheap bed, her nose spraying it with droplets of crimson blood.

'Don't hurt her,' Adonis cried and turned to leave.

'Where are you going?' Thomas said, blocking his way. 'Sit!'

One bodyguard grabbed him from behind, forced him to his knees and placed his head on the mattress. Thomas squatted by his side. 'You're watching the whole thing. You have to see how bets are paid.' The second bodyguard tied Kate's wrists to the bed post and ripped off her dress and underwear. He placed his large hands over her mouth and nodded to his boss. Thomas climbed upon the bed and untied his belt. Kate shook her body to fight him off, only to receive another punch to her face. She felt drowsy as Thomas entered her. Tears ran freely from her beaten eyes. The bed shook and Adonis closed his eyes.

With a grunt, minutes later, Thomas Keravnos fell upon her. Kate could not breathe with him on top of her and her face covered by the bodyguard's hands. She gasped for needed air. Thomas's breath smelled of strong cigars.

Finally, he arose from her. 'Lock him up and have some fun, guys. I'll be enjoying a smoke in the lobby. I've got some business to discuss with the manager.'

'No, no. No more! Leave her alone,' Adonis begged. Thomas kicked him between his legs. Adonis fell to the dusty floor, only to be picked up by the hair. The tall bodyguard with the curly hair dragged him to the closet and locked him in. There, in the darkness, Adonis continued to hear his wife's ordeal. With his head between his knees, he waited. He lost track of time. He placed his ear on the crack of the closet doors. Silence lingered outside the confined space.

Adonis brought his eye close to the dimly lit line separating the closet doors. An empty old-fashioned armchair and a faded painting came in sight. He moved around, trying to broaden his view. Kate's bare feet hung from the old, creaky bed.

'Kate? Kate?' he called out. No reply came. Her stillness scared him. He began kicking the thin-wood doors; his right foot opened a hole big enough for his arm to pass through and unlock the wardrobe.

He froze in shock before the double bed. His wife lay badly beaten; blood and bruises between her legs. He placed his hand over his mouth. He rushed to her side. She was not breathing. He slid off the bed, sat on the floor and cried. Cried like never before. The love of his life, raped to death for a stupid card game.

Voices came from outside. He recognized the high-pitched voice of the manager.

'Is he coming here? Could he be ordered to finish me off? Is that the business Thomas had in the lobby? What if he is with the police? Thomas owns half the department! They will frame me...'

In a state of terror, Adonis did not wait for his thoughts to be answered. His survival instincts kicked in and he stood up. He lifted his light, thin wife and threw her over his shoulder. He made a run for the fire exit; car keys in hand. He plodded down the fire escape, metal screeching following the thud of his steps.

He paused at the corner of the motel. The car park was deserted. His white antique Beetle waited below the tallest oak tree. He dashed at into the open, glad the aging motel had no security cameras. He bit his lips and avoided looking at her face as he dropped Kate into the boot of his prized Volkswagen. He ran back up to the room's window. No one was to be seen. He quickly collected their possessions, chucked in their blue Samsonite and crept back outside.

Funny how the brain can unbury memories when pressured. Adonis drove the dark country road at full speed, his headlights dancing upon tree to tree, scaring sleepy birds and squirrels with his engine's roar. In his mind, a school field trip from years ago played out. Mitsero village. Home to the famous Red Lake. A deep lake colored red by the acid waters provided from the closed-off mines surrounding it. Nothing managed to live in its waters, the tour guide had informed them.

'Perfect! No fishermen, no divers, no swimmers...' Adonis said aloud as he drove by the outskirts of the small village. Pure silence. Long after midnight and the hills stood quiet. He parked at the edge of the cliff with his lights switched off. He untied his brand-new mountain bike from the car's hood and with the gear in neutral, he pushed the vehicle off the edge. The Beetle sky-fell below, crashing upon the cliff's side and rolling into the dark waters with a loud splash. Adonis watched as it sank out of sight.

'*Oh, God, what the hell am I doing?*'

With three hours left until daybreak, he rode his bike through Mitsero forest back to his home. He stayed locked up inside for two days. The neighbors had to testify that he was away for the weekend. On Tuesday, he reported his wife missing. He stated how they argued on the weekend away and how Kate took his car, and drove off, leaving him there. He informed the police that he returned home by bus. With tears, he said that he waited for her to come home. How her phone was switched off and how she threatened to leave him for good as she walked out of the motel room.

Months later, the story of the missing woman was forgotten by the local media and became just another buried file in the overcrowded filling room of the police department.

Ayia Napa, Cyprus
March, 2018

Sotiris Andreou parked his black BMW in the underground parking off his apartment block, in the prestigious area near Nissi beach, one of the island's most celebrated and awarded beaches.

It was his first day back at work after his boss, Thomas Keravnos had died six days ago. His feet ached after standing for hours as a bouncer at Castle Club, having to put up with girls trying to flirt their way in the crowded club and with drunken tourists arguing between them.

At five o'clock a.m., he was alone in the dark, concrete maze. With slow, heavy steps he made his way to the elevator on his right.

A noise from the shadows behind the thick columns caught his attention.

'Bloody rats,' he whispered before gasping for air as the pickaxe pierced his chest. He fell back, his eyes widened in shock. A slim, shadowy figure stood towering him. He tried to focus as the woman came closer.

'Wait! What do you want from me?' he said as blood oozed out of his chest. He felt weak and each breath seemed more elusive.

'Don't you remember me, big guy?'

Her short, brown hair and Greek nose came more into the light.

'Jesus Christ, you're that woman from the motel!'

'Bingo,' she said, pulling out the heavy pickaxe.

'Your husband said you died. He called Thomas and told him to cover up all evidence at the motel and have the manager back his story...'

Those were his last words. The sharp end of the tool came down with force, piercing through his bald skull.

Hours later, a doctor rushing to his car –late again for his morning shift, found the body. He calmly checked for a pulse, wiped the sweat from his bald head and called the police. For the second time in a week, Chief Inspector Demetriou found herself examining a murdered body and contemplating her choice of a career.

'This has to be an underground vendetta,' she said to her partner who stood amazed at the pickaxe sticking out of the victim's head. 'He worked for Keravnos. We need to talk to other employees. Something bad must have gone down and I sense more death is on the way. Especially if Keravnos's men decide to retaliate.'

Her partner stood up straight and rubbed his lower back. His nose twitched, having inhaled the thick, stale underground air that roamed the parking lot, now, carrying a smell of fresh death. 'That's if they have a clue about who's doing all this.'

*****

The news of Sotiris Andreou's death fuelled the media who channelled their top reporters to the 'wiping out the mob' case. On a small island, everything is big news and these murders were huge to the public.

Just two blocks away, Chris Panayi, Keravnos's second bodyguard held his curly hair between his large hands and walked up and down his living room.

'Babe, relax...' his wife tried to reason with him.

'Relax? Relax, she says! I've got a target glued to my forehead and Agnes wants me to relax.'

The Swedish beauty stood up and hugged him from behind, laying her head on his wide, bare back. 'Who has a target on you? The other nightclub owners? They all fear you,' she said and placed a gentle kiss on his shoulder.

Chris closed his eyes, his mind travelling back to that night. He held the pillow down too tight. He just wanted her to be quiet. That night changed him. He turned to his only living relative for help; his grandmother. The Cypriot granny with the silver hair sent him to her spiritual monk for guidance. Chris cleansed his soul and sought redemption, spending his days off helping out at the children's hospital in the nearby town of Paralimni.

'It seems you can't escape your sins. I have someone to see. It's either him or he lied that his wife died,' Chris said, picked up his white T-shirt from the back of the brown sofa and rushed out the door.

Agnes stood puzzled. 'Just be safe,' she managed to yell as the door slammed behind Chris.

*****

Adonis spat out another piece of nail and watched it fall on the Persian carpet. His iPhone with the news sat by his side, keeping company to the opened bottle of scotch. Adonis lit another cigarette. Funny how he never smoked indoors before Kate's death. Now, he flicked the ash on the floor beside him. He remained laying down as the cigarette burnt down to his lips. He fought to maintain his mind calm and empty.

'This is not the time to panic, Adonis,' he yelled aloud as he thought of going to the Red Lake and swimming down to her body.

Twenty minutes later, he heard a car pull up outside. He drunkenly sauntered to the window and took a peek from behind the thick tartan curtain.

'Holy shit,' he said as he saw the tall bodyguard exit the vehicle; his curly hair blowing in the gust of wind coming from the hilltop.

Adonis rushed down the stairs and went down to the cellar. As he heard the doorbell echo downwards, he climbed out the narrow window and made a run for the hill, hoping for the evergreen pines to provide him with cover. Running up the hill he turned to make sure if anyone was following him. He froze in shock. There she was. Kate crawling into the back of the bodyguard's Land Rover.

He rubbed his closed eyes in disbelief. She was wearing her pink spring dress with the wild flowers printed on the back. She loved that dress this time of year. Adonis hid behind an aging fir tree and spied through its broken branches. The bodyguard walked round his property, knocking on doors and calling his name. Five minutes later, he gave up and returned to his car.

Adonis fell back into the dirt as the bodyguard drove out of his metal gate and vanished down the narrow road.

'How is she alive? I should have checked for a pulse... I should have taken her to a hospital... I deserve to die...'

Adonis stuck his fingers into the soft soil and pushed himself up. His head felt heavy; his eyes sore. 'Don't take this as disrespect. Thanks for the cover,' he spoke to the tree as he took a much-needed leak. He pulled up his jeans' zipper and scratched his head. 'Maybe the booze is playing tricks on me. I've been thinking about Kate all week...' he mumbled as he clumsily made his way back home.

Hours later, his answer came through his television set.

'I knew what I saw was real!' he yelled and jumped up from his bedroom's two-seater sofa.

Chris Panayi's death was announced by Chief Inspector Demetriou on the evening news. She was surrounded by reporters and the gang of microphones covered her up to her lips. The victim was shot in the back of his head with his own gun. He was found by the side of the road, dumped by two garbage bins. His car was found abandoned behind an old coffee shop, near a bus stop. Witnesses spoke of a tall, pretty lady with dark shades and a pink dress on. '... we cannot confirm an ongoing mafia vendetta, but we can assure the public that they are safe. Police are interviewing the route's bus drivers as we speak and in combination with our other leads, we are confident that arrests will be made shortly. Thank you,' Demetriou's last words came through his sound surround system.

Adonis exhaled and brought yet another cigarette to his lips.

'*I will not run. I want to see her. I will stay right here...*'

Last Day of March, 2018

Days went past uneventfully.

Adonis never left the house. In self-inflicted quarantine, he lingered through the dark house, living on delivered meals, alcohol and cigarettes.

Dawn came and found him still awake after a night of pepperoni pizza, cheese sticks, Mythos beers and a Lord of the rings movie marathon.

'God, this movie has way too many endings,' he complained as he got up to take another relief trip to the bathroom. He returned to his living room sofa –the new resting place for his pillow and sheets, before the closing credits. As he watched the hobbits sail off into infinity and the next scene cut back to Hobbiton, he leaned forward to take a closer look at one of the extras in the background.

'He looks like the motel owner. Grumpy, old man.'

An idea came to him. *'Could he be on Kate's list? What if this is really just mob hits and executions? It has been weeks...'*

He switched off the movie, went back into the bathroom, splashed cold water upon his unshaved face, rubbed the black circles camping around his eyes and brushed his teeth. In his boxers, he rushed to his bedroom. He pulled up a pair of jeans and took a clean T-shirt out of the closet. Soon, with the morning sun rising behind him, he was in his car, windows down, driving back to a place where he thought he would never return.

An hour later, he scratched his short, thick beard as he turned down the country road leading to the two-story motel.

Few cars were parked outside; only lively crickets breaking the silence of the morning. Adonis parked his vehicle near the entrance and got out of the car, unsure of what to say.

'Hey, remember me? I'm the guy that lost his wife in a poker game and your boss with his goons raped her to death? Listen,

what's going on with your mafia organization? Is it a vendetta? A drug war? Jesus! I'm a complete idiot...'

His thoughts kept him company as he crossed the parking and stepped onto the patio by the motel's main entrance. A loud noise behind him made him jump. A well-fed, though stray, ginger cat leaped out of the overflowing dumpster below the outdoor staircase. His hairs standing straight up as he walked sideways, ready to fend off two approaching enemies. A woman's figure stood opposite him, in the shadows born from the stairs.

'Kate?' Adonis called out, taking a small step towards her direction.

The woman came into the light. 'Good morning, I'm Stella. I run the place. Was just feeding the cats. Looking for a Kate, huh?'

'Erm, no. Not really,' he replied, scratching the back of his head.

The olive-skin woman raised her green shades from her eyes. 'A room, then?'

Adonis watched her right hand slide across her shorts and hide below her black tank top. 'No need to go for your gun. I'm not here for trouble.'

'A gun, sir? What are you implying? This is a legitimate business...'

'I'm not a cop. Nor a journalist. I know this place is where Thomas used to settle a lot of his dirty business...'

'Good morning, Mrs. Areti. How are you today?' Stella raised her voice to cut him off and waved to the old lady strolling on the first-floor balcony. 'Maybe we should take this inside?' she whispered to Adonis.

With the office door closed behind them, Stella exhaled and sat down on her black office chair. 'So, what's your deal?' she said, dropping her friendly tone and lit a cigarette. 'Sit!' she ordered.

Adonis sat in the high-back armchair opposite her. 'I'm looking for the manager...'

'That's me.'

'No, no. The old guy. Short, long grey beard and long scruffy hair?' He left out the 'looks like a hobbit part.'

'What do you want him for?'

'Questions about a night that could be connected to all these deaths.'

Stella blew out a thick cloud of smoke, leaned forward and placed her hands on the mahogany desk. 'Who are you? Did you work for Thomas? I haven't seen you before.'

Adonis shook his head. 'I'm nobody. A fool that got himself in a sticky situation. Please, can I speak to your manager?'

Stella fell back into her chair. 'My father died from a heart attack last Christmas. But, if you know anything about these murders, you need to tell me now. Someone is targeting us...'

Adonis placed his hand upon his forehead. 'You just answered what I wanted to know. I wanted to ask your father, if the murders are drug –related or a result of a vendetta or whatever that went sour.'

'What's it to you?'

'I believe my wife was murdered here last March or at least that's what I thought... I've been seeing her... I don't know... Maybe I'm crazy, but I thought maybe she was the one doing the killings.'

Stella looked at him hesitant of what to say or think of the bizarre stranger that showed up at her motel at the crack of dawn. She blew out another large cloud of smoke and dropped her cigarette to die in an empty ashtray by her phone. 'Did my father kill your wife?' she finally asked.

'No, no,' Adonis shook his head. 'I'm sorry to have wasted your time. It was a far reach, but I was hoping for any answers your father might have had about the three deaths.'

'You're scared.'

'To death,' he replied and forced a smile. He stood up. 'If I'm right, this story will close with my death and you and the mafia are safe. If I'm wrong, then I'm safe to live in guilt and you lot need to find out who is hunting you down.'

Stella did not reply. She watched as the sweaty man rushed out her office. She followed him and noted down his number plates.

*****

Adonis returned home exhausted. His ankles cracked and his knees retaliated as he stumbled up the stairs. Fully clothed, he fell on his bed and in seconds, drifted off to dreamland.

Kate haunted his dreams. Every dream of his, she turned into a nightmare. She rose from the Red Lake and followed him through the dark forest, naked and abused. Blood dripping from her insides and a sharp knife in her right hand. Her eyes were missing. Adonis tried to run, yet branches moved around him, blocking his way. Tall, gothic trees laughed and taunted him. The trees held him down. Kate sat upon him and raised the blade. As its end pierced through his eye, Adonis screamed and found himself awakening in cold sweat. He ran to the bathroom and splashed icy water to his face, wiping away sweat and tears.

'Adonis?'

He froze and looked behind him. 'Am I still dreaming?'

'Adonis?' the female voice echoed around the room. It was coming from downstairs. Adonis stepped back into his bedroom, opened his closet and picked up his baseball bat.

He descended the stairs with care. Barefoot, he looked around as he moved. A smashing sound from the living room made him jump. He noticed the clock above the door. Midnight. He had slept all through the day. He crept into the room and switched on the lights. His wedding photo lay surrounded by pieces of glass. He approached the broken frame and picked up the picture. The smiling faces raising memories of happy days long gone. His gambling addiction made sure their life together lacked joy. As he stood up, his bare foot landed on a tiny piece of glass. It cut through his flesh with ease. He hopped in pain to the armchair by the dirty fireplace. He sat down and pulled out the small glass segment from his skin. Just then, he felt the thin rope run around his neck and he was yanked to the back of the chair. A blow to the head made him lose his senses. He reopened his eyes to find himself tied to the chair, unable to move. The lights were out and only the lit fireplace provided light.

Kate sat in the shadows opposite him. Her feet rested in the light; he recognized her favorite heels.

'Kate... Kate... How? You're alive!'

'No thanks to you,' she whispered.

Adonis began to sob. 'I'm sorry, I'm so sorry. Whatever I say is not enough...'

'You deserve to die!'

'I know,' he replied, thought skeptic with the rasp in Kate's voice. 'Did you kill Thomas and the others?' he asked, hoping she would talk louder.

'All of them. Revenge really does taste sweet.'

Adonis titled his head. 'You're not Kate.'

Laughter came from the shadows. 'No, you dumb bastard. Of course not. Believe in ghosts, do you?'

'Eva?' he asked in surprise as Kate's sister came into the light.

'Is this where we have our movie scene where I describe my plan? Do you need such satisfaction, Adonis?' she asked as she came closer, butcher's blade in her right hand.

Adonis remained silent. 'Just kill me...' he said and bowed his head.

'Not before you answer me. What did you do with my sister's body? She's surely dead, right?'

Adonis raised his head. 'Wait... what do you know?'

A door from the kitchen screeched slightly and Eva turned around. *'Did I leave it open?'*

'Eva, believe me, I had no intention of causing any harm to Kate. I loved her...'

Eva yelled and brought the blade down, chopping off two of his fingers that rested on the armchair. 'Loved her?'

Adonis screamed in pain and looked down in horror at his two bloody fingers lying on the vinyl floor.

'I never trusted you. You made her suffer, day in, day out. The hours she spent crying in my arms, whenever you lost money and had drunk your weight in alcohol. And then, you took her to that shitty motel to be raped. That's your idea of love? You sick fuck, huh?'

Adonis's tears snaked down his pale cheeks. 'How did you find out?'

'As I said, I never trusted you. Your smug face telling the police that she left you, that she disappeared. After months went by and she did not even call me, I knew something bad had gone down. She would run from you, but she would have let me know where she would be going. I visited the motel you said you stayed at and found the manager. I forced him to tell me the truth. I listened to how you sorted a rape night for Keravnos and his two bodyguards. I would probably have gotten more out of him, but I injected him with too much and he went into cardiac arrest...'

'You killed the old man? Well, go on, nurse. Cut me where you know I will bleed out. Guess your profession helped you become a murderer...'

Her laughter cut him off. 'You're judging me?' she said and the knife came down again, chopping off another finger. 'What did you do with Kate? No one knew where her body was.'

'I found her dead. I put her into the back of the Beetle and drove her off the cliff, into the Red Lake.'

Eva screamed and frantically began cutting him. Blood shot up high as she slaughtered him; butchered his body.

Breathless and covered in blood, she dropped her knife and cried. 'I love you Kate... Sweet revenge for you, babe,' she whispered and turned to leave. She gasped for air as she saw the woman standing in the doorway.

'Hi, I'm Stella. Just heard, you murdered my father,' she said, raised her gun and shot Eva between the eyes. 'Don't know about sweet, but revenge is surely a bitch,' Stella said, walked over to the fireplace and threw lighter fluid into the flames and made a line leading to the sofa. As Stella drove off into the night, she saw from her rear-view mirror, the flames devouring the curtains.

The burnt house with the two murdered bodies was the second unsolved case in a row for Inspector Demetriou. She gave her resignation to Homicide at the end of spring. Murders just weren't for her.

THE END

About the author:

Luke Christodoulou is an author, a poet and an English teacher (MA Applied Linguistics - University of Birmingham). He is, also, a coffee-movie-book-Nutella lover. His books have been widely translated and are available in five languages (with more on the way).

His first book, THE OLYMPUS KILLER (#1 Bestseller - Thrillers), was released in April, 2014. The book was voted Book Of The Month for May on Goodreads (Psychological Thrillers). The book continued to be a fan favorite on Goodreads and was voted BOTM for June in the group Nothing Better Than Reading. In October, it was BOTM in the group Ebook Miner, proving it was one of the most talked-about thrillers of 2014.

The second stand-alone thriller from the series, THE CHURCH MURDERS, was released April, 2015 to widespread critical and fan acclaim. The Church Murders became a bestseller in its categories throughout the summer and was nominated as Book Of The Month in three different Goodreads groups.

DEATH OF A BRIDE was the third Greek Island Mystery to be released. Released in April, 2016 it followed in the footsteps of its successful predecessors. From its first week in release it hit the number one spot for books set in Greece.

MURDER ON DISPLAY came out in 2017 and enriched the series.

HOTEL MURDER, the fifth and 'final' book in the series, followed in early 2018.

Luke Christodoulou has also ventured into 'children's book land' and released 24 MODERNIZED AESOP FABLES, retelling old stories with new elements and settings. The book, also, features sections for parents, which include discussions, questions, games and activities.

He is currently working on his next project, a different kind of book, which he is secretive about.

He resides in Limassol, Cyprus with his loving wife, his chatty daughter and his crazy newborn son.

Hobbies include travelling the Greek Islands discovering new food and possible murder sites for his stories. He, also, enjoys telling people that he 'kills people for a living'.

Find out more and keep in touch:

https://twitter.com/ @OlympusKiller

https://www.facebook.com/pages/Greek-Island-Mysteries/712190782134816

http://greekislandmysteries.webs.com/

(Subscribe and receive notice when the next book in the series is released)

Feel free to add me:

https://www.facebook.com/luke.christodoulouauthor

Note to readers:

First of all, thank you for choosing my book for your leisure.

If you have enjoyed the book (and I hope you have), please help spread the word. You know the way! A review and a five star rating goes a long way (hint hint).

For any errors you may have noticed or questions about the story, let me know: christodoulouluke@gmail.com